DISTRICT LINES ···· VOL. III

A Publication of Politics & Prose Bookstore

Editor
Justin Stephani

Editorial Staff
Anton Bogomazov
Jenny Clines
Susan Coll
Leah Kenyon
Rose Levine
Jon Purves
Rhonda Shary

Copy Editing
Jeanie Teare
Richard Teare

Design
Justin Stephani

CONTENTS

ZEAL

ENLIGHTENMENT

DISTRICT LINES

VOL. III •••• WINTER 2016

Drawing by Frans Boukas

An Anthology of Original Local Work

Published by Politics & Prose Bookstore

5015 Connecticut Avenue NW
Washington, DC 20008, U.S.A.
Phone: (202) 364-1919
Email: districtlines@politics-prose.com
Website: www.politics-prose.com

Politics & Prose reserves the right to reprint material in a "Best of" anthology. All other rights revert to individual contributors upon publication.

ISBN: 9781624290718

This book was printed on Opus, the Espresso Book Machine located in the fiction room at Politics & Prose Bookstore. To learn more about printing your manuscript on Opus, visit us online at www.politics-prose.com/opus. To get started printing with Opus, email opus@politics-prose.com or call (202) 349-1182.

Politics & Prose Bookstore
Founded in 1984, Politics & Prose Bookstore is Washington, DC's premier independent bookstore and cultural hub, a gathering place for people interested in reading and discussing books. Politics & Prose offers superior service, a wide range of book choices, and a haven for book lovers.

RECKONING

WISDOM

INTRODUCTION

Zeal. Enlightenment. Reckoning. Wisdom.

While reading and assembling this year's submissions to *District Lines*, it struck the editors that the pieces added up to more than a series of anecdotes and images about our neighborhoods. Cover to cover, these narratives of family, fear, failure and renewal, of moments pensive, funny, and sometimes tragic, span the arc of life.

From childhood excursions to the National Mall and Harpers Ferry, to crises of marriage and career, to the graves of Arlington National Cemetery, many of the pieces here trace personal growth and transformation. They also trace our city's passages, from the changing spawning patterns of fish at Peirce Mill, to memories of the Washington Senators, to the shuttering of Reagan National Airport in the days after 9/11. And then there are of-the-moment snapshots of Washington today: creeping gentrification, lively Saturday nights at a pizza joint, and a comical near-meltdown in traffic.

This year, our staff read blind submissions from more than 120 writers and artists. We were not able to include them all, but every contribution helped this project take shape. We would like to thank everyone for sharing words, ideas, and stories; whether imagined or real, each submission contributes to a larger, collective narrative that is unique to DC.

We hope you enjoy reading our anthology, and that it enhances your appreciation of our region now and for years to come.

—Justin Stephani

ZEAL

FLIGHT PATTERN: ZACKARY

By Gabriella Brand

All during recess, while the other kids perfected
their drop kicks or chased each other through the
climber, the quiet boy simply sat on a swing and
watched the sky, waiting for the stirring and
suck of air as another jet, inbound for Reagan,
glided over the school playground.

Sometimes a teacher said, "Why aren't you
running around?" or "Get some exercise, Zack."

So the boy would get off the swing and wander
across the grass, but he'd never stop looking up.
The planes were part of his day. Like the turtle
in the science room. Like the kind lady who
directed the carpool line.

He read the airline names aloud to himself. Then
he followed with his head, as the jets, one by
one, swallowed the space above MacArthur
Boulevard, and eased down the
Potomac like geese heading south.

He sometimes traveled with his family,
wedged next to the window, his ears cottony-
thick, his mouth dry as a pretzel, going off to
grandma's or holiday, itchy with anticipation.

But being inside and seat-belted, it wasn't the
same. He couldn't take in the whole bird, the
grace of its beak, the determination of its roar.

Here, out on the playground, he liked to imagine
the jets as pterodactyls, wider than a soccer
field, larger than third grade itself.

He wished that the creatures could dip down
and let him ride on their silver backs,
bronco style, his tee-shirt flapping, his hair
blowing and turbulent, his face visibly brave.

He envisioned the city below him like
a puzzle on a table, the toy cars crossing
the Key Bridge, his classmates and teachers
rooted to the ground, not even knowing he was
gone.

THE REFLECTING POOL

By Alexa Mergen

As children, my brother & I each had a wooden boat
to float on still waters of the reflecting pool.

His blue; mine red.
Small brass hooks & eyes held the mainsails coiled. I unfurled
the sail to catch the wind. The boat raced away & I ran after.

No matter the day,
two crafts launched from the same point inevitably
drifted apart. From opposite ends of the park we hauled the toy hulls
from the pretend sea joining up enough to follow our father home.

IN MY POCKET TO KEEP

By Kris Weldon

When we arrive, the National Mall is covered in stalls and stands, one enterprising gentleman selling slices of watermelon for $2 apiece. Dad buys three slices and makes us do the math as we slurp down soft pink pulp.

"How much did we get that watermelon for at the grocery store yesterday, girls?"

"Four dollars," my sister says. She spits a seed to the grass, the shiny flat black disk tumbling from her mouth.

"How many slices do you think he gets out of one watermelon?"

We watch the watermelon man chop and dice his fruit, handing them out in star-spangled napkins. His knife makes a fat, satisfying chopchopchop sound.

"Twenty?" I guess. "Maybe more?"

"What's 20 watermelon slices times four dollars?"

My sister and I glance at each other. "Eighty!" She shouts it first.

"Next year, Daddy's going to get a watermelon stand," my father says with a little nod to himself, voice solemn.

Dad talks about getting a watermelon stand every year, but we never do. Talking about a watermelon stand is the tradition, along with Rocket Pops, fireworks, and our run to the Metro. Actually, selling watermelon would be fun, I think, but I'm happy enough to just eat it.

The afternoon runs hot, that DC-in-July heat that presses you from all sides like you've been poured into a mold, liquid left to sit, until you cool off and become solid again. We wander towards the Washington Monument. I get a Rocket Pop from an ice cream cart and unwrap it delicately, reverently, examining it from each angle. Strawberry, lemonade, blue razz in a rocket shape... Nothing could be more American in my mind. Somewhere in the depths of my 13-year-old soul, I know that slurping up a Rocket Pop is the epitome of celebrating Independence Day.

DISTRICT LINES

13

The 4th of July is always a thick day, stuffed with humid skies and sweaty shirts, an excited buzz charging up and down the Mall. Only the chill of ice cream can cut through it. I savor every lick and bite, July melting the treat in my hands. Blue razz runs down my arm in rivulets, horrifying cerulean veins on my skin. I baptize my sticky arm in the Reflecting Pool, children wading beside me as their parents soak tired feet. On any other day, Dad would tell me not to touch the water, but today the Reflecting Pool belongs to us all. We share it, keep it in the drips and drops that run down our skin, soaking our clothes.

I examine my naked Rocket Pop stick and turn to my sister. "What kinds of keys don't open doors?"

She ponders for a minute, ice cream sandwich trickling to the ground. "Piano keys."

"Monkeys," I frown, reading the red print on the wood. I glance up at her, tucking the stick into my pocket. "Your answer is better."

"Way better. Monkeys have thumbs."

Dad marches us through the crowds and we stake out a spot to sit. Other families have blankets and baskets, tents and coolers. We've brought nothing. It will be easier to run without anything extra in our arms.

We take turns guarding our precious feet of grass, going to fetch funnel cake and lemonade like army scouts. The sky turns a reddish-orange, pomegranate almost, then a deep purple. We keep pressing Dad's watch to make it glow. The crowd hums. They're checking their watches too, I think.

A hush falls, and music begins. I can't tell if it's speakers or just the distant echo of some orchestra playing somewhere else. Then the first firework rips open like a bag of popcorn left in a microwave too long. I can feel the color spreading across my skin, face tilted up to the sky, jaw dropped as the explosions tear through the night. People begin to cheer around us as the national anthem plays, as more fireworks explode and shimmer to smoke.

Behind me, Dad keeps checking his watch.

My heart pounds in rhythm with the fire in the sky. The fireworks begin to flood the black canvas, promise of a grand finish of red and blue and blinding, sparkling white. I know—because I sit beside the Flags of the World poster at school—that lots of countries have those three colors as theirs, too. But I figure they belong to me for one night, like I can put them in my pocket to keep beside my naked Rocket Pop stick.

"Girls," Dad nudges our shoulders and turns. "Let's get to the

Metro."

We follow him through the packed, cheering crowd, a forest of knobby knees and denim shorts, Dad clearing a path. The sky is pounding, but I can't risk turning my head back to watch, losing my father and sister. The music swells, a rising wave. People clap and shout when we reach the edge of the grass. Dad waits, just a second, for us to emerge from the throng.

Then, he runs.

I take a deep breath, push my sister forward, and dash ahead.

I don't need to glance back, to watch the explosions. This is our own grand finale. Our feet beat the pavement, echoing the fireworks. We watch the grand finale in the glass of buildings, the white of sidewalks, the halos of our hair. I skip over a curb as my sister dodges between bushes, Dad far across the asphalt muddy with color. Above us, the world is falling apart into its primary colors.

Strawberry, lemonade, blue razz...

The streets are devoid of cars, vacant of traffic and pedestrians, and we have the yellow lines to ourselves. We're squealing and laughing, breathless. It feels like cats are scratching at my lungs. We'll get to the Metro just as the fireworks end, and beat most of the crowds like we always do. Until then we run, and we put the empty DC streets in our pockets to keep.

SNOW DAY IN WASHINGTON

By Kelly Ann Jacobson

We had a bit of snow at dusk, enough
to make the drivers nervous and the children
hopeful in their inside-out pajamas,
noses making fog along the window
like sticky fingerprints. Collectively
we waited, salt already scattered,
shovels with our empty boots prepared to
waltz us out the door to Narnia, where we
might meet our own White Witch or Aslan
or that neighbor's dog who barks into the
vents and scares the rabbit half to death but
in the snow would seem as innocent as
a pair of circled prints.

We had a foot more snow, and with it
neighborly anticipation cocoa-warm
(not coffee, which belongs to grown ups
and their email flurries, deadlines pushed
like snow beneath the plow). Inches added
as darkness fell and altostratus clouds
continued overhead like bellies of
white whales. We analyzed their wake,
all but praying for a few more inches
or icy roads.

We woke up to the sound of plows
constructing banks and skiing snow
into a compact canvas; we stayed in bed
until the news of cancellations was confirmed.
Yet Narnia seemed far away in light reflected
off the white embankments, and children
hesitated at the whip of winter on their cheeks.

:: DISTRICT LINES ::

16

PLEASE COME BACK
By Leah Kenyon

The 18-wheeler shoved past, a gale of dust and smoke in its wake. The air darkened and shimmered. My family, pedaling steadily far ahead of me on upright Schwinns, winked out of sight. Then the highway started tipping, gently tipping, rising as if to fold me in its asphalt bed.

It must have been my father who came up with the idea of a family bike ride from DC to Harpers Ferry. Daddy's deepest love was reserved for his bicycle. Then came math puzzles, hole-digging, napping, peanut butter sandwiches (unsalted peanut butter, marmalade, unsalted bread), bike trail maintenance, and his family.

He had seven children, two with his ex-wife, Barbara, and five with his second, my mother Linda. Numerically, we were an achievement. Mathematically, less so.

Daddy bicycled to George Washington University every class day (Mondays, Wednesdays, and Fridays) at 5:30 a.m., opening each of our bedroom doors to shout "Goodbye, everybody who's awake!" before pedaling away. At work, he changed into a clean shirt, jacket and tie, fresh and ready to deny clemency to bleary-eyed calculus students during office hours of 6:30 – 7:30 a.m. Then class at 8:00, one or two classes more, and home again to a peanut butter sandwich (triple-decker if he wanted to lose a pound or two, quadruple-decker if he wanted to maintain), a short glass of cold skim milk and the cryptic crossword. Daddy had tenure.

At dinner he sat at the head of the table, letting the conversation flow over him, saying only: "Could some kind soul please pass the salad?" (Or whatever it was he wanted, but never butter or salt.) He let the need to assert himself build until he would inevitably announce something like this to the rest of the table, usually during the pause before dessert: "I have the following idea: for every X, let there exist a Y of equal or lesser value, such that…"

I sat on his right, so it was my job to supply him with scrap paper made from Xeroxed exams with which to illustrate his proofs. Then I had to listen and pretend to understand. The others were free

17

to resume bragging about basketball and arguing over the right to call "short stops" before passing the salt and pepper to someone seated farther away.

Meanwhile, before Daddy had finished even one step of his proof, I was lost. OK, I understood that there were X's and Y's, and that any x was greater than or equal to any y—but as he must have known, I was still struggling with long division. Still, I kept my end up by interjecting "Yes, I see" or "Explain that last part again?" occasionally, and remembering to smile and say, "Thanks—that was interesting!" once he was done. Daddy would reply, "Yes, wasn't that an elegant solution?" He then rewarded my attention by allowing me to pick any date in history, after which he calculated aloud until he came up with the corresponding day of the week.

From such minds, great and terrible ideas are born.

The plan was to take two days biking up to Harpers Ferry, spend a week at the Potomac Appalachian Trail Club guest house (conveniently abutting a graveyard at the top of a hill overlooking the town), then spend two days biking back.

Even Daddy didn't expect Naomi, age five, Miriam, seven, or me, nine, to do the ride in one day. Rachel, 14, might have been able to manage it, but decided instead to keep her parents and younger sisters company. Only Amos, who at 17 wanted as little to do with his family as possible, went on ahead. He arrived at Harpers Ferry the same day, while we spent the night at a motel about 20 miles away.

Daddy had rigged Naomi's bicycle to the back of his with a couple of pieces of heavy rope, but the rest of us had made it on our own. Television was our sweet reward. We didn't have one at home—TV was for rich people and motel guests. We watched re-runs of "Happy Days" and "The Brady Bunch." I was so unfamiliar with the medium that I mistook comedy for high drama, but savored it deeply nonetheless.

The next day came: a little downhill stretch along Route 15, a longer stretch of towpath along the C&O Canal, then over a bridge and into Harpers Ferry. There was plenty to do once we got there—we explored the graveyard (so many dead babies!), climbed around the ruins of a burnt-out church, visited the decrepit wax museum featuring John Brown, militant abolitionist, and gorged on French fries and frozen chocolate custard for lunch. The junk-food ban was temporarily lifted—even root beer was not out of the question.

All week the weather was lovely, a little cooler and less humid than Washington in July. We swam in the Potomac until somebody mentioned leeches, went on hikes and history tours, and curated our rock collections. We played sardines in antique shops and took afternoon bike rides to the neighboring town of Bolivar, West Virginia: "Welcome to Bolivar—Please Come Back." We slept soundly despite the lack of traffic noises. Then, on the morning before we had to leave, I woke up and wondered why the room was spinning.

I stayed in that spinning room all day while everyone else hiked and toured, too feverish, dizzy, and disoriented to join them, too apathetic even to wish for frozen custard or a root beer float. Except for the thumping in my head, the house was quiet. Mommy came back to check on me at lunch—nothing a little soup or ginger ale couldn't cure, in her opinion. Also in her opinion, root canals and childbirth were easily endured without the help of painkillers or sedation of any kind.

That night, my parents gave me a choice: I could go back on the train alone, taking my bicycle with me, or bike back with the rest of the family. I had a few questions: "How am I going to carry my bicycle? How will I know where to get off the train? How am I supposed to get home from the train station? Can't Rachel or somebody come with me?"

But a sick child was not part of my parents' equation, and there was no elegant solution.

They presented a united front, as always. "If you're really that sick, you can take the train. The rest of us will be biking back, so you'll just have to ask someone for help with your bicycle once you get on. Talk to the conductor, I'm sure he'll be happy to tell you when you've reached Union Station. Just ask for help if you don't know what to do—someone will be able to tell you. Or you can bicycle back with the rest of the family, but let us know before dinner, because if you're taking the train we have to buy your ticket tonight. Now, train tickets cost a lot of money, so you should be sure you're really too sick to ride back—you might feel better tomorrow morning."

In Plutarch's account of ancient Sparta, sickly babies were thrown off Mount Taygetus and healthy children subjected to whatever grueling physical tests the Spartans could devise. My parents were proud upholders of this tradition. When I was one year old, I was abandoned in the middle of an archery field during a snowstorm, accidentally I am told. A stranger took me to the Rock Creek Park police station a couple of miles away, where I was eventually reunited with my family. When I broke my collarbone a few years later, my parents left it untreated for several days until it occurred to them that Leah's refusing to raise her arms above her head was perhaps not because such was her tiresome whim—that it might indeed be one of the few occasions a doctor was called for. You will probably think that the snowstorm abandonment story would have left me kindly disposed towards strangers, and that the rest of my experience would have taught me that strangers were perhaps a better source of help than those who shared my own blood. But I was a shy child—asking for help was not in my nature. I chose to bike back with the family.

It was hard work keeping the bicycle upright, keeping my legs pedaling up hills and across bridges, while all the time the world spun round so fast, doing its best to throw me off into the universe. I could almost see the stars.

Now came the stretch of Route 15, uphill this time, with its hot smoky air and trucks that came looming up beside me, then muscling past. Goodbye everybody who's awake. The highway started tipping, gently tipping, as if to fold me in its asphalt bed. Goodbye everybody who's awake. Then I heard something, a voice far away. A quiet voice, a gentle suggestion: "If you faint, you will die."

I thought about that.

"If you faint, you will die." And I realized I was the one making the suggestion, only it wasn't a suggestion anymore, it was a command.

I wanted to faint, I wanted to die.

I wanted to live.

I wanted to live more than I wanted to faint, or to die.

X is greater than Y.

21

FIREBOAT ON THE ANACOSTIA

By Sally Murray James

The red tub toy of a boat
chugs up our city river
wide and tidal here and
on days the trash has drifted out
a source of green relief. Just shy
of the 11th Street Bridge
an unlikely twirl sets in
vessel pitched against current
odd in this realm of bollards
and barriers but yes one jet
of dubious water quality rises
and then uncountable parabolas
dissolving into spray and plash
each particle distinct
and yet unsortable
weary river mixed
with burnished light
late now its brassy heat
burned off. In our euphoria
we find a primitive relief
the ancient choice to side with land
rescinded wholly for a moment
by three firemen at play.

GO FISH

By Lee Sturtevant

Just where the trail by Peirce Mill goes under Tilden Street, where it's wise to stay to the far right of whichever direction you're walking because the bikers can't see around the bridge abutments, a father was pointing down into the creek, where it eddies into a little cove: "Look son, look at the fish."

I look, too, and a school of them—small, silver, pointing upstream—are vainly braving the swirling backwash.

Hey, little fish, I think, just ease up, float downstream a little, then go up the other side, where the fish ladder is.

The boy can't see the point of watching a bunch of fish never getting anywhere, and picks up a stone to throw farther out into the creek.

I walk on upstream. A man is taking a photograph of a pregnant woman posed a bit beyond the cascading falls that a hundred years ago stopped the pregnant alewives and herring from migrating upstream to spawn, as they always had. The falls—foaming and noisy—stretch across the creek but weren't built for the mill, to help grind grain or anything useful. No. They were conceived in 1906 to provide a scenic and pleasant ambience for a teahouse near the mill. Maybe my grandparents went there for a Sunday outing, although it's a long walk from Mount Pleasant and I'm not sure they would have sprung for a taxi.

Some years ago, it became evident that the fish weren't making it to their ancestral spawning grounds, so for a while each spring, optimistic volunteers formed a bucket brigade, to pass the fish above the falls.

It finally took the Woodrow Wilson Bridge, environmental requirements, cooperation—and of course money—from all the local governments to allow and encourage the fish to swim back to where they started.

So the fish ladder around the falls was built along the creek's east side, with its angled entry and 15 gentle baffles allowing the fish to jump up a level, then rest, then jump to the next level until they were out into the creek—making their first run through the ladder in 2007.

"By the time they get out, they're pretty tired," explained Bill Yeaman, the Park's Resource Management Specialist.

A jogger stops to watch fish emerge. "They fight to do it, don't they? Like bicyclists, they help each other."

Because it's a nice spring Sunday, I walk farther upstream, just past the Boulder Bridge, where the creek bends against a looming bank of grey boulders and dark trees. It tumbles over a series of carefully placed rocks, soft rushing water that can even be heard from the trail above on weekends when there's no traffic. These are step pools. They may look random, Yeaman explains, but they are a precise series of openings, at different levels, so the fish can move upstream regardless of the water flow. A lot of heavy equipment and sandbags and engineering created these pools.

Following the creek north, past Military Road and the log cabin, off to the side, I stop at the historic vestige of the other man-made impediment the fish couldn't get past for so many years.

In the zoo, along Klingle Road, Porter Street and farther north, fords were built so carriages could cross the creek. The only trouble was, once the automobile took over, the fords had to be paved and raised so the cars could cross more easily. But not the fish.

The park preserved one historic ford—Milkhouse—and you can walk just up to the edge where the old road meets the water. The ford's deep enough now for the fish. When I was young, it was pretty shallow but it didn't feel like it.

In the summer, going north out of the city, I'd start whining almost when the car started. Please please please can we go through the ford? Please please please.

The parent would roll eyes, make no commitment all the way out Beach Drive. Then the car would slow, ease gently about halfway into the water and stop. Out I'd jump, close the door, grab the handle, and the car would start up again. The cold water always hit my legs with more force than I expected as it pushed past me, with the car now adding its splashing wake, clear enough to see the rough pavement that was scratching my bare feet—all the way across the ford to the deep forest on the other side. Then the parent eased the front half of the car up the bank, and stopped. I opened the door and slid back in, wet feet, wet legs, wet skirt, big smile.

I'm sure all those families enjoying their tea overlooking the waterfall at Peirce Mill a century ago didn't think about spawning patterns. Neither, later on, did I. So I'm sorry, fish, for all your generations who were never born and never spawned. Your creek was such fun, and back then, we didn't know.

ENLIGHTENMENT

FICTION

"WHEN SORROWS COME"
By Zoe Johnson

Act I

T he play that year was "Hamlet." *O, that this too, too solid flesh would melt, thaw, and resolve itself into a dew.* We, the teenage actors of the Shakespeare Theatre Company's Advanced Camp, would be performing it at Harman Hall. Not on the big stage, as I'd originally thought, but on the lower level, in a wide, wooden space, with pillars, curtains on the back walls and no specified stage. When I'd first arrived, I was disappointed by the lack of grandeur, the absence of a capital-T Theater.

"It's just…bare," I'd said to Zara, my best friend who was also in the play. "It feels irreverent." In my three years or so of school musicals, I'd come to see Theater as sacred. The stage was a church; the actors, priests; lines, prayers—though to whom, I knew not. I hadn't yet learned that you can pray anywhere, to anyone, for any reason, without the prayer losing its potency, its holiness. Prayers were prayers. Especially when it came to Shakespeare.

Zara and I were Shakespeare dorks. The kind that knew meter like other teenagers knew rap, the kind with favorite versions of each play, the kind who could recite speeches upon speeches, scenes upon scenes, and often did—in public and with fight choreography, if possible. Among our favorites were the first Kate/Petruchio scene of "Taming"—*Come, come, you wasp. I' faith, you are too angry. If I be waspish, best beware my sting*—along with the Romeo/Mercutio fight, of course, and basically all of "Midsummer." Though the lovers' quarrel required four actors, we could always make do with just two. And yet, for all our dramatic flair and theatrical whim, we found that the best Shakespeare was late at night, lying on our backs in the grass, whispering to one another as we stargazed: *For night's swift dragons cut the clouds full fast, and yonder shines Aurora's harbinger; at whose approach, ghosts, wandering here and there, troop home to churchyards.* It was poetry, that was all. Just poetry.

I ruminated on this during our morning exercises, as I lay on my back, knees together and pointing towards the ceiling, in what our director called "constructive rest." It was comfortable, surprisingly so; as I relaxed, my limbs seemed to melt into the floor, and with my eyes closed, it felt like I was floating. I was supposed to be clearing my mind of thought, but I was too excited, and it wasn't going well.

My best friend lay just to my right, long dark hair splayed over the floor behind her head, halo-style. It was our second week of rehearsals—only 10 days left till the performances—and without looking, I knew she was biting her lip. She was stressed. Anxious. As always. Thinking about it made fear flare up in my stomach, and I quickly returned to focusing on my breathing. *The weekend is two days over,* I thought, trying to be calm, trying to relax, *and I am two days begun.*

Assuming an beginning can be the end of yourself.

Act II

The weekend had been hard, to say the least. Zara had always been nervous, but Saturday was the first day that we had, at last, understood her nervous temperament to be not just a personality quirk but a disease. The diagnosis, somehow, made it real. Not that it hadn't been absorbingly, disturbingly real before—the panic attacks made that all too clear—but a diagnosis meant treatment meant therapy meant stigma meant fear. I looked into her mother's face, that Sunday, and knew that the diagnosis didn't mean healing: it meant with certainty that something was wrong. Which I'd known, all along. In a way, I guess, I was glad to share the burden of the knowledge with someone else.

So was Zara. She didn't want to take medicine, but was glad to have the option; didn't want a therapist, but realized it might help; didn't feel comforted, but felt recognized. Real. Like she had been floating high above the ground—far from reach, far from help; out of control, just drifting—and now, the clouds had parted. She was no closer to landing than before, but at least now people could see that a ladder needed to be built, a helicopter found, if she was ever going to get back to the ground.

Or at least, that was what I thought. She seemed happier. More at peace. But I never really knew. Ours was a friendship of few words—and most of them were Shakespeare's. The closest I came

27

to saying what I was feeling, that whole weekend, was when we were practicing our lines.

"*Doubt thou the stars are fire; doubt that the sun doth move; doubt truth to be a liar,*" I said carefully, testing the words on my tongue, "*but never doubt I love.*" I looked at her at the last phrase. Our eyes met, and there was a pause. I wanted to say something about the past weekend—about how it had been hard but things would improve with time, about how I was proud of her for starting treatment, about how much I cared about her. She took a breath. I wondered if she knew what I was thinking.

" '*O dear Ophelia,*' " she prompted me. I thanked her, and continued.

Now, when we came out of constructive rest, she took a minute to roll over, lie on her side staring into space, before looking up and meeting my eyes. It was lunchtime. Normally, we took half of it to wander around DC and eat, and then ran lines for the other half. Luckily, we were both pretty good at memorization. We had years of practice. I was playing Polonius; she was Horatio. Our characters fit us, I thought. I was pedantic and funny, caring but tight-lipped. Zara was reserved, playful at times but generally in control—*unless she isn't*, my traitorous mind submitted; *you just don't like to think of her like that*. The images rose: Friday night. Zara sitting on her bedroom floor, holding her knees, quaking. Eyes wide, mouth open, gasping for breath.

"Pizza?" Zara asked, tilting her head quizzically. I knew I was looking at her too protectively. I shook it off and took her waist, giving her a side-hug as we walked out the doors.

We ate in the atrium of the Portrait Gallery, as we usually did. The beautiful open space—all grays, but soft, and filled with a raw, shivering light—made us pensive, ready for the afternoon of rehearsal. She finished eating first, as usual, and started scribbling something on her napkin. She loved doing that—it reminded her of artists sitting in cafes in the 1920s, discovering that the meaning of life was not, in fact, death, but killing themselves anyway; reminded her of noble love, gentle life, fierce fight in the face of the truth about life. But the thing about napkins is that they are easily ripped, easily broken, I thought. Love is fleeting. The only truth is in glancing moments.

See? Pensive. I was sure Zara was writing something similar—not in subject matter, necessarily, but in the same vein. It was who we were.

Act III

As the show approached, and Zara's treatment commenced, a sense of waiting arose. But not a patient waiting. A desperate waiting; a deep, conscious need for fulfillment, for the cathartic release that only the conclusion could bring. *No more; and by a sleep to mean we end the heartache, and the thousand natural shocks that flesh is heir to. 'Tis a consummation devoutly to be wish'd.* But I did not want anyone to die or to sleep. That was, in fact, the exact thing to be avoided.

The doctors agreed to start slow: just therapy, for now. Medicine later, if at all. But the revelations were still coming: The panic attacks had been more frequent than I'd realized, that she slept less than her parents knew, that the anxiety was not just a passing phase, but a reality. Zara would say things offhandedly like "Oh, I can't remember the last time I cried"—and then continue with, "but it might have been yesterday." I got the sense that she was just learning to finish the sentence.

Meanwhile, I did research. Anxiety disorders were prevalent but debilitating. In a way, I was strangely glad that they weren't as unusual as I had thought—it was better than Zara being alone. Understanding was low, and so were options.

And the rehearsals continued. We were officially off-book, lines memorized, and fluid on our tongues; the show was almost entirely blocked, and the emotional effect of the play was getting more and more intense. "Hamlet" was a tragedy, and a pretty hardcore one, too. We'd been encouraged over and over again to open our chests to the pain, to the rollercoaster of emotions, and more and more of us were getting good at riding it, at letting the tears come.

I died early on, but I was also playing a courtier at the end, so I got to come out again, which was sort of nice. As Zara—or, rather, Horatio—was left standing over all the dead bodies, I got to mourn with her: We wrapped our arms around each other's backs, aching, grieving. The fights in the last scene were pretty great—like five people died, all in epic ways—but I was reminded, suddenly and soberly, that we were witnessing a massacre. When another friend brushed my back in passing, I flinched.

"You okay?" he asked, startled.

"Yeah, yeah," I said. "Fine."

The thing was, I *knew* Zara, knew her late-night cravings and deepest desires and hidden fears, her profile and birthmarks and profoundly beautiful elbows, her laugh and her somber and every-

29

thing in between. The fact that there was something within her that I couldn't understand made me feel powerless—powerless to help her. After years of friendship, where we could cheer each other up with just some chocolate or a new book or a walk in the park, there wasn't much I could do for Zara anymore. And I knew this was selfish—more than ever, I was realizing what an enormous gift it was just to have a body that didn't sabotage my everyday life; I knew that my best friend was suffering more than I would ever understand and that her suffering was really the only thing that should concern me and my own suffering at seeing her suffering was inconsequential by comparison—but my heart was the only one I had. And it was hurting a lot.

That morning, I'd asked Zara to describe anxiety to me. Everything she'd said so far was so foreign to me. Zara wrinkled her brow and said, "It's like…there's another organ in my body, whose only function is stressing me out. Like if something happens, in the same way that your eyelids shut automatically to keep dust out, that organ panics. And I panic too."

I said, quietly, "That sucks." And Zara laughed. God, how I relished that. She laughed.

Act IV

There'd been a midnight—an aching one, a ready one, a teenager kind of midnight—when we'd walked, steady unsteady, down to the reflecting pool. Actually, it wasn't just any midnight. It was the midnight ushering in the fifth of July, wiping away the stains of fireworks that still lingered on the sky. And it was dark, and the pool was beautiful, and Lincoln was looking down on us, and so was MLK. Zara dared me to dare her to swim: to strip and swim. So I did, and then she dared me to swim, too, and so we both did.

It was hard to explain, but we loved being naked, and we loved being naked together. Or maybe it was just hard to explain to others. To us, it made perfect sense, or at least, I assumed it would've if we'd ever discussed it. I wrote a poem, once, about the time we opened all the windows in my room—there were four—and lay naked on an air mattress during a thunderstorm. The winds had passed over us, cooling and heating us, bringing with it the metallic scent of rain, the burning taste of lightning, the sheer ecstasy of thunder, and we felt like gods, open as we were to the world, to the universe. Showering together was a different kind of joy, but a joy nevertheless; the casual familiarity at chatting while we shampooed our hair and washed the skin behind our ears, the companionable way in which we stepped around each other, politely acknowledging but not dwelling on the beautiful bodies that were ours.

So we were mermaids that night, too. It was probably illegal—probably very, very illegal, actually. But King Hamlet was dead, and Hamlet would be too, eventually, and Zara's panic attacks hadn't stopped, and there were many terrible things in the world. *When sorrows come, they come not single spies, but in battalions.* So we were mermaids in the reflecting pool, because why not. That was what I was learning from the whole experience: why not. Love was fleeting, illness was pervasive, poison thrived in the most innocuous places, and the only truth was in glancing moments.

Exactly.

Act V

Already, it was show week. It was afternoon, and we were rehearsing in our costumes for the first time. Zara sported casual men's garb; me, an old-fashioned black and white suit, the kind my grizzled lawyer uncle wore to his court cases. We sat backstage together, hands linked, as we waited for cues, and we didn't dare talk.

It started off slow, when it happened. The play was pretty far along—already partially through Act V, though the final act was one of the longest, so that didn't mean much—when Zara started dropping lines. I stared at her back. They were lines she knew. But she had been biting her lip before she went on, and her hands had been shaking, and when I asked how she was doing, she said—in jest, I thought—"Alas, poor Yorick." Just that.

Now, it wasn't just her hands that were shaking. It was her arms, up to the elbows. Those beautiful elbows. It was stupid. *I knew him, Horatio.* And Zara was panicking, her breath coming in shorter and shorter gasps, like hiccups but more severe, as she struggled to inhale. Our director moved towards her, but I was already there, my hands on her back. At my touch, she exhaled hard. For a moment, it was quiet.

Then she gasped again and again, tears in her eyes, hands at her mouth, and I knew how it hurt her, how her lungs were burning, how scared she was. I made eye contact with the director, and she nodded. I pressed my fingertips into Zara's back, and she ran like a startled rabbit. *Now cracks a noble heart*, I thought, when I turned

31

and saw the rest of the cast watching, wide-eyed. I hated myself, but I still thought it.

When I found her, she was sitting on the curb, counting cars. Her breathing had slowed, but it was still hiccup-y, still reaching, as if grasping for something just out of reach.

"I didn't—" she said, and I said, "I know."

And we sat. Counted cars.

When we came back in, everyone else had changed back into their regular clothes to finish the play. The director moved quickly to intercept us.

"You don't have to—" she began, and Zara said, "I know." Funny, how we always said that, when we didn't really. We didn't know anything at all. She took her place, and I mine.

And as I waited for the bodies to pile up, I thought about Zara. About my best friend. Everything I needed was caught in her jaw, her big sweatshirt, her laughing, laughing eyes. But now, as the dead lay at our feet, there was no joy on her lips. She knelt—bending slowly at first, then falling fast—and I did, too, slipping my arm around her shoulders as our director had taught me, only two weeks ago. We stayed there, eyes shut, pressing into one another, and cried for everything we had lost.

WILDFLOWER WALK

By Deborah Hefferon

Vernal pools of knobby tree root reflections,
home to gurgling frogs, skipping like stones
across the forested surface. Skunk cabbage
leaps up along the water's edge - a green
so bright I fish out my sunglasses. Virginia
bluebells clang open as the sun climbs. May-
apples raise their tiny parasols, trout lilies spread
mottled leaves, Christmas ferns unfurl. Like time-
lapse photography, spring ephemerals flash
before me. I duck beneath the spice bushes, step gingerly,
slow my breaths in the tidal cycle of Rock Creek's early April.

SHY SUPPLICANT

By Pamela Murray Winters

Montgomery Blair High School, 1977

Dear sweet Thetis, Mrs. Wubnig said. We were reading
the *Iliad*, and she'd given us each a role. Apparently I was motherly.
I, who wanted poems instead of children, who'd have tied her tubes
sooner than smoked a cigarette, who nevertheless loved naming
characters and plants. I was in it for the syllables. Maybe she'd seen
my books of baby names. (David: "beloved or friend.") There were

many Davids; you were the most golden. What did you become?
Jeff, our Achilles, grew his first beard at sixteen, played Tevye
in *Fiddler*, and now works in Hollywood. (See IMDb.) Today
I envision him sulking in his tent in 1977 A.D., his long legs
crossed, hairy knuckles wrapped around an achy foot. Like war,
the classics can be a long slog, less romantic than you'd think.

Feet get cold, and ankles wobble, and the funny boy dies,
stabbed by a trick, and several fail to reach their potential.
Gawky name, Thetis, for a Nereid who never learned to swim
and dropped out of Swarthmore and managed despite it all
to have a house with cats and to forget or half-remember and wake
with the sun. You were one of many passing chances. You were

the golden David, the one who was Zeus, last in the alphabet,
first on Olympus. On Tuesday I think I was to beg you to spare
my hulking thespian son. I remember the phrase *supplicate his knees*.
I think that's why on Tuesday I stayed home with cramps. And so
your knees went unsupplicated and my crush fell away. For another David
was Poseidon, and this David had red hair and talked to me.

:: DISTRICT LINES ::

34

MY MANIC PIXIE DREAM GIRL

By Vanessa Steck

Jane Eastman was my manic pixie dream girl.

We were two of the eight lifers in our class of 25 at Park Street School, seniors who had been there since preschool. We'd gone through to kindergarten in the Early Childhood Wing, crossed over to elementary, started wearing uniforms. In sixth grade Jane examined the uniforms for upper school and decided that merely wearing navy plaid skirts instead of navy plaid jumpers was unacceptable. She crashed a board meeting with a goddamn powerpoint. They didn't give in to all of her demands, but Jane explained that she had asked for more than she expected so the Board didn't feel like they were completely acquiescing to an 11-year-old. Park still uses those uniforms.

I tell you all of this so that you can understand Jane. She could talk a homeless man out of his last dollar, an addict out of her last fix.

Senior year was a very big deal at Park. We had always gone on lots of trips as a class—it was Park's hallmark, and in grades one through eight we had gone sailing, skiing, and climbing, and monthly we'd hopped on the Metro to visit a museum or garden or monument or historic building. We had been to Monterey in ninth after studying the ocean, to Italy in tenth to see the ancient world, to Egypt in eleventh after studying the Middle East. But senior year was Capstone.

It was the only class we had all together, and it was the last period of the day. Our other teachers worked in the whole high school, but the Capstone teacher, Mr. Neille, worked only with seniors. He had designed the program a zillion years ago, when he first started teaching at Park out of college; the year we had him he was 68 and legendary. We'd had all kinds of teachers—funny, cool, strict, old, those that actually taught and those that gave out worksheets—but we had never had a teacher like Mr. Neille.

The first day Mr. Neille gathered us in the senior commons.

"Tomorrow," he intoned, "you will begin the process of choosing your Capstone site. You will do so carefully. You will not do so based on what malls or sports teams or anything else with limited worth are nearby. You will do so based on passion."

He paused and looked at the gaggle of girls who were scribbling in notebooks and whispering. "There is no need to take notes while I speak, ever," he said. "I will not be giving you facts that you must memorize for some test."

We had never, ever heard an adult say the word "test" with such disdain.

He went on for the full hour, touching on choice as an important concept—with a casual foray into reproductive freedom that went by so quickly many of us didn't notice until later—and talked about how as privileged kids we had an obligation to choose well. We had never, in our entire school career, sat and listened to a teacher for a full hour. Our normal classes were 45 minutes, but even then, no one lectured the whole time: there was always a project, a quiz, a discussion. But we sat listening to Mr. Neille. We couldn't not. He was magnetic.

The next day he spread out a huge map on the commons rug. It had, labeled, every single historical site, museum, monument, interesting geological formation, anything of note, within a six-hour drive. We spent the week studying the map, researching the locations; on Friday, we handed in our top three choices. The following week, Mr. Neille put us in charge of planning the logistics. He gave us the budget, our lists, the time frame—two weeks—and told us to put together a schedule in which we could rent a bus, drive to one site on each person's list and be able to spend three to four hours there, and camp at night.

It was a ridiculous thing to ask 25 teenagers to do. For one thing, we all wanted to advocate heavily for our top choice, but of course in order for the trip to work, most people would have to settle for their second or third choices. Not something we were used to. And it was an obscenely complicated logic problem.

It took us ten full class periods and we only managed because Jane took charge, telling us to stop being morons and focus. So it was that two weeks after we'd been given the assignment we handed an itinerary to Mr. Neille.

We had all been surprised at Jane's choice. She alone had put down the same site for slots one through three, because it was already in DC. We kept asking her, don't you want to go somewhere?

She would shake her head. She wanted the Vietnam Memorial,

and that is what she got.

At last, the fourth week of school, Mr. Neille took his usual place in the commons and told us the details

"You have all chosen a site," he said. "Your job, between now and May 10th, is to learn everything about that site. Not some things. Not most things. Everything."

He paused and looked at us.

"This is, of course, an impossible task. You are not magic, you are merely mortal, and therefore, cannot know everything about anything. But you may not stop until you feel that you have learned everything. Do you understand?"

We nodded. We were rapt. I realize it may seem silly to you, now, but for us it made perfect sense.

"And then," he informed us, "you will all have one hour, before we arrive on your site, to present it to us. Now. I cannot stand boring. I don't care how you do it. Film a movie, do interpretive dance, make a diorama. It must tell us the most salient and interesting information about the site, and it must not be boring. It must be accompanied by a paper exploring what you've learned, and of course, you'll have to cite your sources properly and all of that—"

Someone asked how long the paper had to be.

"Oh for god's sake," Mr. Neille said. "What do I care how long the paper is? As long as you need it to be and no longer."

"But—" most of us said at once.

"Every year," Mr. Neille sighed. "The papers are anywhere from 20 to 80 pages most years. But there is no requirement. As long as it needs to be and no longer, and I do not want to discuss it any further."

And that was all he said about that.

So we went and attacked Capstone. Oh, we did the rest of our classes, too, our trig and physics and Literature of Africa and AP World Civ and History of DC and AP Calc. We finished our college apps and waited anxiously for results. We went on five weekend camping trips so that during Capstone we'd be able to set up the tents, cook dinner and breakfast, and cope with weather. We visited the Holocaust Memorial Museum, many of us for the first time, and it was one of the few experiences at Park that humbled us. We went to the National Gallery with sketchbooks. We delivered Christmas gifts to low-income kids. We maintained our solid win-loss records in lacrosse, field hockey, baseball, and soccer. Mostly, though, we were excited about Capstone. We spent an hour every day on it. We did research on the origins of our site—I had Times Square, some-

DISTRICT LINES

what of a cliché for Capstone—and we looked at the history, went to the Library of Congress as a class several times to look at original documents. We read poems, short stories, essays, novels about our sites. By March, most of us had started working on our presentations. We helped each other navigate the technology.

Except for Jane. Jane worked alone.

There was a subtle shift in her that year. After all this time—and the endless talking about it—still, I cannot pinpoint what it was. She was just a bit different. But I was a 17-year-old boy and all of the girls seemed mysterious; it was just that I only loved Jane. I did notice—we all did—that Jane stopped hanging out after school. She was still effervescent most of the time while we were in class, while we walked to the nearby strip mall for lunch; she was Cordelia in our fall production of Lear, she wrote her column for the newspaper, she participated in discussions. But except for school events we did not see her outside of Park.

Much later, when the press got ahold of the story, librarians from all over the city would report that Jane had spent whole afternoons in their children's rooms, asleep at the table with books fanned out around her.

Capstone was fabulous while we were on the road. It was exactly as much fun as you'd expect—for us. Perhaps it was less fun for our teachers, chartering a bus with comfy seats, TV screens and wifi to take all 25 of us and four teachers (Mr. Neille, obviously; Mrs. Earle, science; Mr. Maynard, art; and Ms. Compagnucci, English) on a road trip. We visited one or two sites a day, viewing the presentations on the way. The part that most of us had been looking forward to was the road-trip, and it did not disappoint; we liked the camping, eating s'mores every night, and having lots of time to play stupid games. But we were surprised at how interesting the presentations were. We were 25 very smart kids with a lot of resources, and we had, collectively, found some truly amazing stuff, put together some genuinely innovative work.

Jane went last, when we circled back to DC. It was the final day of our trip and we were exhausted but satisfied. She had asked to be allowed to present at the Wall itself, and Mr. Neille had said sure. He liked Jane. Everyone did.

It was spring in DC, hot and a bit muggy but with enough of a breeze to make it bearable. We were in our summer uniforms, though Mr. Neille clearly thought this was foolish and didn't care how we wore them; our other teachers gave us a break, too, ignoring untucked shirts or rolled skirts. We spread out in the grass near the memorial and Jane stood in front of us. She looked radiant. We had all noticed, and some of us had even discussed it amongst ourselves, that she was in a better mood on this trip than she had been in the previous weeks; she seemed more bubbly, more herself.

The rest of us had had multimedia presentations: a Prezi, a webpage, a movie. We had photographs, snippets of writing, time-lines, models we had made. We could press play, let them run on the screen in the bus.

Jane just talked. She ran through the basics of the Vietnam War, said it was a stupid, arrogant war. She segued easily into just war theory, Iraq, Afghanistan, the importance of supporting soldiers while holding them accountable. She ran through the Wall's inception, Maya Lin and her contest. Then her voice grew husky and slow. She sat down in the grass and talked to us about trauma.

Jane said it was like being haunted. She described flashbacks, the sudden jolt, the overwhelming sensory experience of remembering. Even without specifics, she captured the feeling better than anything I've read or heard since.

I glanced over at Mr. Neille. We knew he'd been in Vietnam; he'd mentioned it occasionally. I was shocked to see tears tracking. I'd never seen a teacher cry. It was terrifying.

Jane finished talking at the exact end of an hour. Steadily, she said her presentation was over but she was going to go walk on the wall—none of us realized, then, that she said "on"—and we could come. She stood and walked away, her canvas messenger bag swaying at her hip.

We followed her to the Wall. We'd been there before on previous field trips, of course, but all of us were suddenly solemn and thoughtful in a way we had never been on our trips. We all ran our hands over the endless names, felt the heat of the black stone rising into our skin.

Then someone, I do not remember who, said "Oh my god."

I have a picture of Jane from that moment. It's my favorite of Jane. And the one that I hate the most.

She is standing on top of the Wall. She must have just stepped on at the lowest point. It's very narrow up there, but Jane had been a gymnast and she had excellent balance. She made it several yards before the crowd noticed her en masse.

I snapped the picture just then. She's wearing the summer uniform she pioneered: a baby blue polo, a mint-green skirt. Unusually, she wasn't wearing shorts under it: we could see the shadow of her pale legs, her translucent skin. Her hair, flaming, tomato red, hung loose past her shoulders. She was somehow barefoot, toenails the same verdant green as her eyes. She looked completely calm as the crowd gawked, our teachers yelled, her peers cheered, the park rangers approached.

She was the most beautiful thing I have ever seen.

Then she reached into her messenger bag and withdrew a gun.

None of us had ever seen an unholstered gun in real life. We knew shootings happened all the time, but we did not live in that place. None of us could have told you what a gun sounds like when fired right next to you.

We can now, though.

It happened very fast. Jane pulled the gun smoothly to her mouth. She stuck it in, leaned a bit so that she started to slip off the far side of the wall, pulled the trigger. It was less than ten seconds from the time she reached into her bag to the time we heard a blast that burrowed into our bones, the final thud as her body hit the grass. I won't describe the rest of the scene. You've seen movies.

The only clear memory I have after that is of Mr. Neille, at 68, leaping over the shallow part of the wall, saying "Oh. You beautiful, foolish girl. Oh, Jane."

I don't remember much else.

It was a huge story, obviously. In a media studies course I took in college, someone called it a sexy story, and I confess that I punched him. In the mouth. They found her browser history; she had visited websites that described the best ways to commit suicide, researched the angle at which to cock the gun. They never did figure out where she got the gun, but it would not have been hard.

Her sister Kara, 19 and at Yale, drunk-dialed the *Times*, said she thought something bad had happened to Jane the previous fall, but she didn't know what it was: Jane wouldn't tell her, even when she'd visited Kara the weekend before we left for Capstone, bringing gifts of her favorite poetry books. Her sister Lucy, 15 and a sophomore at Park, said Jane had been quieter until the last three weeks, when she'd taken Lucy to dinner and given her some favorite novels. Her parents said nothing to the media, or to us. We knew Jane's parents, a little bit, in the way we knew everyone's parents. We had seen them at events, at occasional playdates when we were younger. At the funeral, they sat in the front row with Kara and Lucy and did not speak. My parents sat on either side of me, my brother next to my dad. I wasn't particularly close to my parents, though I liked them well enough, but that day I felt overcome with gratitude for them. My mother held my hand the entire time.

We graduated because we had to. Mr. Neille gave the commencement address: as a class we had demanded him, rather than the speaker Park had chosen. He spoke about choices and courage and the nearly unspeakable sadness of losing our dream girl. He told us not to let it be unspeakable. He added that he would be graduating with us: Jane's choice, he said, was no one's fault, not ours and not his, but he could no longer lead Capstone.

He gestured to her empty chair, with her graduation cap and gown on it, a picture of her. "Live large, the way your comrade did," he said, and began to weep; the head of school took over.

We moved on. There was no other choice. We kept in touch via Facebook and Class Notes, trying on adult personas. We have had 100% attendance at every reunion.

I moved away after four years at Georgetown, following Lindsey, who became my wife after we had both finished graduate school. We tried West Coast living, but I wanted to go home. After our twins were born, Lindsey agreed. The boys started Nursery at Park the year our daughter was born; now I watch her enter the upper school in her mint green skirt and baby blue polo, and I pray that she will not be, in the admittedly romanticized way we all still think about our manic pixie dream girl, too fragile and too beautiful to live on this earth.

Her name is Charlotte Jane.

FOLLOW THE WHITE RABBIT

By Courtney LeBlanc

I saw her again,
the girl with the tattoo.
I spotted the spade inked
on the back of her arm and realized
it was the same woman I'd followed
only days prior.
Today the train was crowded,
strangers pressed against one another
in an awkward introduction.
She faced the door, the ink
that had entranced me turned away.
When the train doors opened
and she exited
I moved slowly, suddenly reluctant
to learn the words that had given
me such chase, afraid
of the disappointment
they may contain.

AFTER THE MARCH

By Emily Sernaker

Everyone went back to the their days in the city
wearing bright red shirts with white writing that
said STOP MODERN DAY SLAVERY. They
were everywhere – the park, the monuments,
Chinatown. Shopping in Urban Outfitters, ordering pizza.

I thought this is how other people must feel during
PRIDE or BREAST CANCER walks. In between
shiny beads and folded pink ribbons. This is what
it is like to see others who carry a shared identity or
private concern. Washington DC gets tense

before it rains each summer. It is muggy and stalled
and feels stuck in a brick of heat. It is hard to tear
away from or know what to do. And when it does rain
it does all at once and our bodies ease and voices say
good this is good, now we are being honest. This
is what we need, what we wanted all along.

SATURDAY NIGHT: JUMBO SLICE

By Melody Rowell

I t's midnight. Two women, one in hot pants and tall boots and the other in a skin-tight mini dress, dance unabashedly in the middle of the floor. Illuminated by technicolor flashing lights, they sing along to the steel-drum-infused hip-hop music blaring overhead, pretending to ignore the stares from the men and women encamped along the sides. One man stands against the corner of the bar, next to a sign advertising "Africa's Most Wanted CD"—available only at this establishment. After a few minutes, he takes off his green apron and joins the women on the dance floor, thrusting his hips and pumping his hands in the air.

No, this isn't the latest and greatest nightclub DC has to offer. It's Jumbo Slice, the hole-in-the-wall pizza joint smack dab in the middle of U Street. Here, pizzas the size of tractor tires are sliced into pieces the size of a grown man's torso, stacked under a warming light, wedged into too-small boxes, and sold at $6.50 a pop to the District's revelers.

Mohammed, a slight, soft-spoken man in an olive polo, tells me that he's been the manager of this joint since 2001. In 2011, the spot got bought out, but he was retained to run the newly christened Jumbo Slice. When I ask him his favorite part about managing this restaurant, he smiles proudly and says, "The atmosphere. I created this." After he watched other restaurants on the street fold, he knew he had to do something different. "People are out partying, they get hungry, they need something to eat within walking distance," he says. "But I have to give them a reason to come in." So with some strategic lighting and a bumping sound system, Mohammed made his run-of-the-mill pizza place an extension of the DC club scene.

As it turns out, few people can resist the temptation. Not a single person walks by the narrow glass storefront without slowing down to look in. Most who do cross the threshold twist and gyrate their way to the counter, like a drunken wedding party getting intro-duced at the reception. The wall to the left sports a pasted-on black-and-white poster of Audrey Hepburn in "Roman Holiday." The wall

44

to the right, a rudimentary, painted caricature of a grinning Italian chef.

Both decorations seem affected, given the ethnic diversity of the employees of Jumbo Slice. Patrick, a three-year veteran of the pizza counter, counts on his fingers the countries represented: Jamaica, Tunisia, Burkina Faso, Mali, Jordan, Niger, Morocco. He grins, revealing a twin set of dimples, when he says his fellow employees are his family.

The enthusiasm is hard to resist. A well-dressed couple who look to be in their mid-40s tell me they smelled the baking pizzas a block away, and once they heard the music they knew they had to come in. They seem divided on the quality of the pizza, but agree they'd even come back in the middle of the day—music or not. A group of young women are huddled together in another corner of the restaurant, going through what seems to be a well-rehearsed ritual of sprinkling a slice with Parmesan, folding it up, and eating it without ever setting it down. They tell me they come here once, maybe twice a week. Through a mouth full of cheesy dough, one tells me, "We go out, we party, and we're STARVING, so we always come here. It's SO GOOD." A hipster British couple, new to the area, say they had friends insist on a visit to Jumbo Slice. "We heard we had to come here," the wife tells me. The husband mentions that they were just at Busboys and Poets for a drink and decided to check off the Jumbo Slice box too. When asked if it has lived up to the hype, they look at each other and laugh. "It's pretty good," the wife says. "If I were drunk, this would be the best pizza of my life."

By 1:15 a.m., the eyes of the incoming visitors are progressively more glazed. Two men giggle as they stumble out, peeking into their boxes as though a secret prize hides within. A huge man in a black down vest in spite of the heat, serves as both bouncer and buser—keeping the floor free of debris and the women free of harassment. Mohammed and I watch the impromptu dance party unfolding before us, and I ask him the hardest part of this business. "The cost," he says without missing a beat. "It's an expensive place to be, and the food is expensive to make. I've watched a lot of other businesses close around here."

"There's no danger of that happening here, is there?" I ask.

He laughs and shakes his head. "No. No."

It's a small comfort in this transitional city. As long as people like pizza, drinking, and late nights, Jumbo Slice will be here to welcome them with piles of pizza and Africa's Most Wanted CD.

MISS KITTEN AT BLUES ALLEY
By Cary Kamarat

Down the alley, where jazz lovers find a reason for the blues,
down Blues Alley, in the faux-glow of gaslight gone electric,
pools of whiteness spill, over all the hues of red brick
holding up the night, above a shopfront quaint but hot—
promising something Big, for that lovin' Georgetown crowd.

Step lively 'cross the tiles, and wet your whistle just a bit,
then find a table meant for two where four lovers squeeze to please
and there she is—she's on the menu, between that Sarah Vaughan Filet
and Bugnon's Ginger-Mango Brie it's Miss Kitten's Catfish Po' Boy
sweet and brown, served all crispy, 'leven-fifty, what a deal.

Down the alley where jazz lovers find a seasoning for the blues
down Blues Alley, there's a boudoir high above the café noise.
On those wide and wobbly stairs where stars descend then fly to rest,
sits Miss Kitten, scared as always steppin' out on that icy stage.
But she can warm it to a hot pink, and she knows it. So she stands,

pushes off then purrs and snuggles down the steps all time-worn
quiet as a hidden past, in a cloud of French perfume.
Here comes Miss Kitten—someone whispers—*she likes million-dollar daddies.*
Someone said she found one too—that's because there is a God.
Now the memories ebb and flood, voices hush, 'round the room.

From plantation to Manhattan, to the White House, London, Paris,
Kitten stepped out of her alley long ago, paid her way.
So she rises to the stage now where the hangin' spotlights sizzle,
looks across a padded shoulder, lets a Cheshire smile just beam,
through that midnight lamé sparkle, under Cleopatra eyes.

You know she'll laugh out loud, if she catches you in love, and wanting more—
that's when it really begins to flow and spin around that cabaret floor
at Blues Alley, for that lovin' Georgetown crowd.

64 SQUARES

By Harold Stallworth

A single bead of sweat dripped off the tip of Jamahl's nose and fell onto a vacant square on the chessboard. The tiny splash broke his concentration.

Sitting opposite Jamahl was an older Dominican man, Celso, wearing a tattered Georgetown T-shirt, an olive green messenger bag slung across his body. A small crowd had gathered around their table, watching intently as Jamahl pondered his next move. He reached for his remaining knight.

"You sure you wanna do that, my friend?" Celso asked, flashing a smile.

Instinctively, Jamahl began to draw back his hand and reconsider his strategy, but it only took a fraction of a second for the smug tone of Celso's comment to cut through the fog of exhaustion clouding his brain. Ten-hour shifts dulled Jamahl's senses; on days like this, which was to say at least six days a week, his old lady, Patricia, likened him to any number of black characters on "The Walking Dead." Cornbread. Pookie. Sincere. He'd always felt uneasy about such crude, lazy comparisons. This had less to do with Patricia's race, which was thoroughly white, and more to do with the fact that she was conflating 50 years of black film with some stupid zombie show. This is what was running through his mind before Celso's smug comment.

"Man, I don't need no help," Jamahl snapped at Celso, unconvincingly. "Worry 'bout your own side of the board."

As the crowd chuckled in unison, Jamahl gained a brief surge of confidence. He reached for his queen and dragged the piece back to the corner of his side of the board.

Without hesitation, Celso hunched forward and plucked his rook between his long, slim fingers, slashing across the length of the board with a confidence that bordered on disrespect. "Checkmate," he said cockily.

The crowd winced in admiration before dissolving into the light bustle of Marvin Gaye Park. It was the first weekend of spring that felt like summer. The park resembled an old Coogi sweater: narrow sidewalks burrowed through an unnaturally green expanse of grass, where thick pairs of brown and yellow thighs pushed slowly behind baby strollers; purple and orange emanated from the sky as the sun set over Northeast. Whereas the young men grazed aimlessly, their older, wiser counterparts sat slumped on the benches, smoking cigarettes, surveying their surroundings. At 28, Jamahl was too old for grazing and too young for surveying. He fancied himself a loner, inclined to self-help books, minor league baseball and the like. "Bougie shit," as Patricia called it. And naturally, the game of chess, with all its imagined and yet-to-be-imagined intricacies, fell under the umbrella of Jamahl's bourgeois pursuits.

Jamahl had always been in love with the idea of being something of a self-trained chess prodigy, a grandmaster of the ghetto. He'd taught Patricia how to play during the honeymoon phase of their relationship, back when she would've done just about anything to gain his favor. He still remembered the admiration welling in her eyes as he explained the strength and stipulations of each piece on the board. But once she moved into his apartment just three blocks north of Marvin Gaye Park, on the east end of Hayes Street, their long nights of red wine and chess tutorials soon turned to long nights of red wine and petty accusations, arguments over nothing.

One evening, after a particularly trying day at work, he asked Patricia, "How could you possibly have an even passing knowledge of Sonny Carson, and somehow still think he's a character on 'The Walking Dead'?"

"How," she returned with an air of derision, "do you continue to be such patronizing asshole?"

It wasn't until meeting Celso on the W4 bus one afternoon on the way home from work that Jamahl became truly obsessed with the game of chess. Twirling a vinyl scroll that looked like a tiny yoga mat, the Dominican man boarded in Fairfax Village and squeezed into the window seat beside Jamahl.

"What's that?" Jamahl asked, his eyes trained on the scroll as it danced between the man's hands like a cheer baton. It appeared to be tied with a drawstring from the waist of a pair of jogging pants or basketball shorts.

The man gently tugged on the drawstring and 64 squares spilled over his lap. "Chess," he said with a thick Caribbean accent and a hearty laugh. "I try to teach the guys on my crew, but they don't have no patience, man. You play, my friend? Are you a man of patience?"

The man was every bit as black as anyone Jamahl would expect to encounter at a family reunion, yet he sounded—in Jamahl's estimation—Puerto Rican. He looked to be about twice Jamahl's age. In his early 60s. He was just bald enough to be considered bald. Thick eyebrows that seemed to never arch, stubborn in their geometry.

Jamahl was so taken aback by the accent that he responded to the question with one of his own. "Where you from, man?" he asked, skeptically.

"Puerto Plata."

Jamahl was only half-right.

Celso introduced himself. He said he was a foreman for a local construction company that specialized in historic concrete restoration. He was currently assigned to a project in Georgetown, repairing an impossibly steep set of stairs that became famous for being featured in "The Exorcist." To corroborate, he jerked a safety helmet bulging from his messenger bag to show Jamahl the company logo emblazoned on its sides.

Jamahl gave a gracious nod of approval.

In order to fit the helmet back inside of his bag, Celso had to empty the rest of its contents into the crown of the helmet, one handful at a time, scooping clumps of loose screws, chess pieces, foam ear plugs, and miscellaneous debris until the bag was nearly empty. Only then was he finally able to work the helmet back inside his bag. While he was struggling to snap the bag closed, a pawn fell to the floor and bounced into the aisle, landing under Jamahl's outstretched loafer.

"I play a little chess," Jamahl said as he doubled over and retrieved the piece.

"You any good, my friend?" asked Celso.

"Never been beaten."

"C'mon. Really?"

"I mean, I don't play much anymore. I might be tad rusty."

"You never forget, my friend. It's like riding a bike."

"Yeah," Jamahl said as he handed the pawn back over to Celso. "That's one way to look at it."

From that point on, almost every evening after work, Jamahl and Celso met in Marvin Gaye Park to play chess to an audience of grazers and surveyors and baby strollers. Sometimes the young women manning the baby strollers invited Jamahl to their apartments for home-cooked meals. And once Patricia caught wind of their advances, she took care to never miss another match. She'd rush home from Aiton Elementary School, where she worked as a guidance counselor and intramural volleyball coach, to freshen up and change into something more flattering than her usual uniform of black slacks, white blouse, and billowing cardigan sweater.

So today, after the crowd dissolved into the light bustle of Marvin Gaye Park, Patricia saddled up beside Jamahl and helped gather up the chess pieces, stowing them in Celso's messenger bag.

Quietly fuming over his defeat, Jamahl extended his hand across the board in concession, as he always did after losing to Celso, which happened far more often than he cared to admit. No matter how many lunch breaks he spent with his face buried in the spine of Stefan Zweig's *Chess Story*, no matter how many times he curled up on his couch to watch "Chess Fever" or "Searching for Bobby Fischer," Jamahl could never push Celso to anything more than a stalemate, and even then there was always the illusion of Celso having the upper hand.

"Another game, my friend?" Celso asked.

"No," Patricia said tersely, dumping the last of the chess pieces into Celso's bag.

"He ain't ask you," Jamahl said. He looked up and around, trying to get a feel for the time. Day was giving way to dusk. "We should be going," he continued, addressing Celso but glaring at Patricia. "I'ma catch up to you tomorrow though, man."

Celso stood to his height and jokingly saluted the couple. "Tomorrow," he assured them.

Jamahl and Patricia walked toward their duplex on Hayes Street, bickering the entire way. Celso headed the opposite direction, down Division Avenue.

The following evening, on the way home from work, Jamahl didn't see Celso on the W4 bus. This didn't strike him as particularly unusual; more often than not, Celso would beat him to the park by at least half an hour.

It was 8:00 p.m. before Jamahl realized that he'd been stood up. "It's not like him to no-show," he said to Patricia, who was busy picking the lint from his disheveled polo shirt.

"Maybe he had a hot date," she said, pursing her lips.

"He ain't have no goddamn date," Jamahl said, amused by the idea. He pulled his phone from his pocket and dialed Celso.

Celso picked up almost immediately. "Jamahl," he said, sullenly. "I need your help, my friend. How fast can you get down here?"

"Down where? What's going on, man? You aight?"

"My place," Celso said before hanging up.

Jamahl was stunned by the exchange that had just occurred. He didn't even know where Celso lived. He assumed it was within walking distance of the park, but Celso had traveled more than 1,300 miles on a rogue banana boat for the opportunity to lay bricks at the feet of trust-fund kids. He imagined that their ideas of walking distance were worlds apart. Jamahl had just finished explaining all this to Patricia when he received a text message from Celso, presumably the old man's address.

Driven by both curiosity and concern, Jamahl and Patricia walked eight blocks down Division Avenue, then hung a right on East Capitol Street. On the way, they speculated about the magnitude of Celso's misfortune. Their theories grew more implausible with every block, as they one-upped each other in sly competition.

Jamahl said, "I bet he's getting evicted and needs help moving his stuff out."

Patricia squinted her eyes and scrunched her face in consideration. She tilted her head at an angle that revealed a thick vein running up the side of her neck, then flicked a stringy wisp of hair back behind her shoulder. "Maybe he's getting deported back to the islands," she said.

"He might owe money to some Dominican drug lord."

"Or," Patricia interrupted. "He could be facing jail time for a crime he committed years ago. There's no statute of limitations for murder or terrorism. I learned that from 'The Walking Dead'."

Jamahl was certain that Patricia had picked that tidbit up from last night's episode of "Law and Order," but he let it slide. He couldn't remember the last time they'd spent so much time together with so little arguing.

"Maybe Celso started selling drugs after he got an eviction notice," Patricia said excitedly. The words tumbled from her lips without pause or foresight. "But he ended up having to murder his plug, and now he needs us to help him dispose of the corpse! Otherwise, he'll be deported back to a Dominican jail!"

They both laughed because it was such an awful thing to discuss in jest. Then they stopped laughing just as abruptly. They walked in silence for a while.

When they finally turned the corner of the address, they found Celso sitting on the stoop of a rowhouse, nursing a glass of something brown. Celso waved them inside.

"Cognac?" Celso offered.

Patricia passed.

Jamahl obliged.

While Celso was off in the corner playing bartender, Jamahl took in the living room in a few slow, sweeping glances. In spots, beige paint peeled from the walls like sloughed skin, exposing the original chalk-white finish. The hardwood floors were blanketed with mismatched wool rugs. There wasn't much in the way of decor—no paintings, no flower pots, no throw pillows. Just a pair of leather chaise lounges circling a glass coffee table, a shallow stack of vinyl records propped against a huge floor-model television, and a lone section of a German shrunk masquerading as a liquor cabinet.

Celso returned with another glass of cognac. "Please," he insisted as he handed the drink to Jamahl. "Have a seat."

Jamahl and Patricia hesitated, somewhat puzzled by Celso's hospitality, seeing as how there were only two seats to be had among the three of them. But once Celso plopped down in one of the chaise lounges, they followed suit and perched on the edge of the other.

"I'm headed back to the Dominican Republic in a few days," Celso said. "Already booked my flight and everything."

Jamahl's eyes ballooned as he waited for the other shoe to drop, half expecting Celso to admit that he'd buried the corpse of a Dominican drug lord in his backyard.

"So, you are getting deported?" Patricia asked.

Celso laughed into the rim of his glass. "No," he said. "I'm selling this place to a development company. They offered me twice as much as it's worth. Five times more than I bought it for in the '80s. That kind of money can go a long way back home."

Celso gestured toward the German shrunk. He asked, "Wanna take the bar off my hands?" he asked. "Liquor included. I'd hate to let good booze go to waste."

Jamahl and Patricia looked at each other and shrugged in agreement.

Celso clapped his hands. The sound echoed loud throughout the underfurnished living room. "So it's settled then," he said. "I'll leave the key under the mat on the stoop. Stop by whenever you have time. I'll be busy running errands for the rest of the week."

Jamahl, relieved to learn that his morbid predictions were way off-base, took a generous gulp of cognac. The liquor warmed his chest going down. He leaned from the chaise lounge to get a closer look at a cluster of picture frames propped on the coffee table. In one photograph, a cute, snaggle-toothed little girl posed with a soccer ball underfoot. In another, a young woman wearing a wide smile and graduation gown hoisted a certificate to her chest. Celso was only pictured in one of the frames, cradling a baby in his arms—judging by the coordinates of Celso's hairline, Jamahl guessed the picture was about as old as he was. Jamahl remembered Celso mentioning his daughters in passing, but the old man had always spoke of them in the way that art buffs tend to romanticize classic works: like fond, distant memories. In turn, Jamahl had always envisioned them as such.

Patricia scooted forward until she sat shoulder to shoulder with Jamahl. She plucked the photo of the snaggle-toothed girl off the coffee table and fawned, emitting a half-gasp, half-grunt in the way that so many women do in the presence of adorable children.

Jamahl said, "We're gonna miss you, old man."

"Me too," Celso responded as he reached down, picked up his messenger bag from off the floor, and started digging out his chess pieces.

Jamahl's pulse revved up and his mind started to race as he plotted out how not to blow this last chance to claim victory over Celso. He briefly pondered throwing the game and leaving the old man undefeated, then wondered if Celso was planning a similar act of mercy.

Patricia gathered up the frames showcasing the snaggle-toothed girl and her impossibly cute siblings to make room for Celso's chessboard. Then she took to the floor, Indian-style, so as not to crowd Jamahl. She wasn't seated for long.

"Checkmate," Jamahl said, in disbelief. The word crawled out of his throat and hung in the air like spring pollen.

Jamahl turned to Patricia to see the familiar gleam of admiration in her eyes.

"Checkmate," Jamahl said again.

IN THE BISHOP'S GARDEN

By Anne Harding Woodworth

Latin names on signs
are propped beside the plants
of yellow, blood-purple-blue blooms,
some whites, some reds,
as if a force were trying
to teach us wanderers
something ecclesiastical
with words like *oculus Christi,*
lachryma Jobi,
and in with the herbs, *Ocimum sanctum.*
Lathyrus odoratus, too,
but the fragrance in a garden
is the unseen, unheard
past participle of flower language.
The garden speaks
without the written word today,
without saying "should, should learn,
for chrissake you should learn
the names of all this bounty."
Why alien words on our tongues
in the face of all this beauty?
Why write the distance
between us and the flower
nourished in hoed earth?

NONFICTION

SUNSET LIQUOR

By Natalie Murchison

W hen I cross First Street NW headed east on Florida Avenue, the sun is setting, and Bobby is half outside, propping the door open with his back, trash bag in his arms. I was going to stop anyway, so this is good.

"Hi Bobby," I say. He doesn't want me to touch his hand because it's wet with paint. I gather this from his smile. The first time I met Bobby I was suspicious of that smile. Now I'm not, though it sometimes burns so brightly that by comparison, my own response feels sluggish and dull.

Inside Sunset Liquor, the air vents, once their natural aluminum shade, shine wet with orange paint. Bobby smiles in their direction. Two kids no taller than my waist walk in. Turning toward the door, Bobby pauses. The boy is a head taller than the girl, his sister I assume. They head straight to the chips. The boy grabs cheese puffs; the girl grabs Doritos. The girl's coat engulfs her like a massive nylon shell.

Welcome to Sunset, the neighborhood liquor store. Less than 200 yards from my house, it is the place to go for wine, beer, vodka, whiskey, coke, grapefruit juice, candy bars, pickles in sealed baggies, chewing tobacco, flavored cigarillos, do-rags, and more. Many days after work, I pick up a snack or drink and chat with the owners, Bobby and his cousin, Baljeet.

"Y'all work here?" the tiny boy looks at us.

"He does," I point to Bobby.

As Bobby moves behind the cash register, the boy lifts the chip bags above his head. After the boy doles out his cash, he turns to me.

"Excuse me, miss. Do you have a dollar so I can buy a drink?"

"No," I say instinctively.

My response elicits no reaction in the boy, not surprise nor anger nor longing. He just turns back to Bobby, who is doling out his change. Bobby's reactions are as slow as an old man's, though he can't be much older than 40.

What did I just say? My bag is fat tonight; it holds two jackets, a book, headphones. My wallet is at the bottom. I dig and pull it out.

"Here you go," I say, handing the boy a dollar.

"Thank you," he says. His face maybe brightens, but if so, only the slightest of degrees.

He pays for their chips and now walks the few feet to the Coke cooler.

"Can I have a dollar?"

I look down. The little girl is looking at me.

"No," I say, once again from instinct. The girl retreats to the Coke cooler. Propping open the door, her brother considers his options.

What is wrong with me? In my wallet lies another one dollar bill.

"Here you go," I say to the girl.

"Thank you," she says, a thin layer of politeness coating her otherwise monotone.

At some point, a man I don't recognize packs up the ladder near the fresh paint. Bobby introduces us. The man is new, started on Wednesday. The new man is quiet, with kind eyes. He has a long face with delicate cheekbones that taper into a stubbly, pointed chin. I think he's Ethiopian but don't know for sure. While the kids shop, the three of us make polite conversation—Bobby, the new man, and me.

I moved to the neighborhood four years ago. In the Craigslist post, my landlord described the street where I now live by its proximity to Big Bear. Big Bear, a cafe in an ivy-covered townhouse, portended development and change. Now, Big Bear is only one of a dozen attractive establishments.

The neighborhood is called Bloomingdale, and within it, each block varies. Some house recent arrivals; on other blocks, families have lived their entire lives. Liquor stores like Sunset have prospered here for decades. Their range of goods varies; some of the North Capitol spots sell laundry detergent and canned goods alongside the beer racks. Plexiglass separates clerk from customer in about half of the stores. At Sunset, Bobby removed the plexiglass several years back. Come closing time, he locks the front door, then slides a steel door vertically over it. At various points, graffiti has riddled the steel, but now it's clean.

The first time I went to Sunset, Baljeet sat behind the register. When I approached her to checkout, she asked me questions in a manner that struck me as Zen-like, detached. She chuckled at some of my answers. Meanwhile Bobby leaned against a wall, hands in his pockets. He spoke less but smiled more. He reminded me of an acquaintance I had who, while intelligent, lacked the force of the analytical, the constant picking apart of everything. Instead, Bobby said hello and goodbye as though operating in a deep and mellow bliss. My visit lasted an unexpected 15 minutes. When I returned the following week, I stayed even longer.

Sunset offered proximity to the entire neighborhood, not just the Big Bear crowd. We all show up, it turns out, for alcohol and snacks. Many of the area teenagers have known Baljeet their entire lives. Often during my visits, the entry bell would ding. "Hey Mama," the customer would say as they walked in. "Hey baby," Baljeet would answer. When an old resident's visit ended at the counter, I would listen as they talked with Baljeet. Before long, I found myself jumping into conversations. It felt good to talk to neighbors, to set aside boundaries that would have otherwise been drawn had we passed on the street.

Inside Sunset, it's easy to differentiate new residents from the old. New residents zip around more. We keep Alamos Malbec and DC Brau on the shelf. I am a part of this group. But spending time at Sunset, that identity's foothold slipped. It seemed as though the neighborhood and I were not such distinct entities after all, that we could mingle. Over the years, I have spent a lot of time at Sunset. The visits were never planned. They were sustained by the sensation of balance I felt afterwards. Some people get to know their neighborhood by doing volunteer gardening or coaching a basketball team. I hung out at a liquor store.

★ ★ ★

The boy returns to the cash register with a lime soda and extends the one dollar bill.

"That is $1.75," Bobby says, arms crossed.

The boy looks at me. I shake my head. I mean it this time. He retreats to the cooler.

Now the girl approaches the counter with a half liter of flavored club soda and her one dollar bill.

"That is $2.50," Bobby says.

The girl looks at me. She can't be older than five. Covered in the tiniest braids, her head is slightly larger than a Texas grapefruit.

"Maybe you two can put your money together," I say.

As the kids sort through the Coke cooler, Bobby waits in front of a bright orange wall. To his left is a metal shelving unit stacked with wine. At the top (I've glanced before) the bottles are as much as $100. I doubt anyone but thieves notices them. The rest of the rack is $15 and under.

"My wife is having hard time," Bobby says to me, smile dimming.

I wasn't going to ask. Last I visited Sunset Liquor was two weeks ago. Bobby's wife, who has suffered a string of non-diagnoses, had just been rushed to the hospital. Back home now, she spends her days in bed.

Later, after I've said bye to Bobby but before I head home, I will stop by the other cash register, atop a mini flight of stairs, where Baljeet is working. In a hushed voice, she will ask how Bobby's wife is doing today. She did not want to ask Bobby herself, though they've now spent a few overlapping hours together.

The new man is behind the cash register. The boy sets down two Arizona Iced Teas.

"Two dollars and 50 cents," the new man says.

Bobby is standing behind the kids now. For an instant he looks like he's protecting them, like he could be their father.

"It's okay," Bobby says, waving his hand. The new man collects their bills.

"Can I get a bag?" the boy asks.

"Five cents," the new man says.

"It's okay," Bobby says before the boy has a chance to look at me.

The new man rips off a black plastic bag from the roll of bags. Into it the boy drops the drinks, both his and his sister's.

"Do y'all live around here?" I ask the boy.

They do. I want to ask them more questions, but I don't want the boy to think he owes me now. He looks up at me, says "thank you" again. Then he and the girl walk out.

One day, I googled Sunset Liquor on a whim. As Sunset lacks an official online presence, the references came in dribs and drabs.

One immediately caught my eye. "Sunset Liquor," the headline began, "destroying the park at First and Florida."

Reading that headline, a storm cloud gathered in my stomach. I clicked.

"It was a beautiful, sunny Saturday," the article started. "On Florida Avenue, drunks urinate publicly and drink from paper bags. Where are they getting the alcohol?"

Sunset Liquor.

Then Sunday rolls around, the article continued. Sunset is closed. At the park, kids are swinging and playing ball. The drunks are nowhere to be found. Sunset Liquor is destroying the neighborhood's growth.

In the comments, there was rhubarb. Many people agreed. The owners of Sunset are getting rich off the down-and-out. "Forget liquor stores; what we need is a good grocery store," someone wrote. "Or how about a tavern?" posted another. A place where you can drink a beer indoors. Waste stays off the streets. Loiterers migrate. The area gets cleaner, safer, less gritty.

"A tavern?" someone responded. "You want to replace a liquor store that's been here longer than you have with a tavern? Seems a bit racist."

The person did not appreciate the remark. This has nothing to do with race, they wrote. After a while, I shut my computer. I let the thoughts swarm around me.

Nothing about gentrification is straightforward, I think whenever I remember the article. Although maybe it is, only as a gentrifier I try to complicate it. Since the comment thread began over five years ago, lots of bars and restaurants have opened in Bloomingdale. Meanwhile, Sunset Liquor is going strong. Bobby now works seven days a week; the Advisory Neighborhood Commission approved Sunset to do business on Sundays. The store's exterior now includes an ATM and also a giant chalkboard, with inspirational quotes next to the weekly specials.

When I think about the neighborhood, I see so many layers. There's the store improvement grant that Bobby won, made possible by local taxes. There are those who routinely purchase singles or stagger outside Sunset waiting for a friend. There are the tavern patios, draped with twinkle lights and packed with young professionals. There are the hairdressers who, after 50 years of business, wrote in their farewell notice that they were closing due to "'gentrification' and mixed emotions." There is the Wednesday before Thanksgiving, on which Baljeet every year lugged pots and platters of homemade

Punjabi dishes from her Maryland home, ready to serve to whoever passed the store.

There is this one ordinary evening at Sunset. Though a few years have passed, it still flickers in my memory.

Outside, it has grown dark. The new man, jacket in hand, asks Bobby if he can go home. "Of course," Bobby says, "See you Monday."

It is now just Bobby and me, Baljeet in the back. I will stay a little while longer, although my stomach growls. I will listen as Bobby talks about the permit that he is waiting on from the DC government so that Sunset can be a deli. The deli will turn out to be an ill-fated plan, but we don't know this at the time. A menu, inspiration, from New York Deli on North Capitol, is tacked on the wall. Bobby hired a man named Jimmy John to secure the District licenses, but Jimmy John has stopped returning Bobby's calls.

"It was a risk," Bobby shrugs.

He paid Jimmy John up front, but only $1500. It could be worse. Bobby will give Jimmy John through the weekend. Then, he will try someone more expensive, a licensed architect this time.

Before I go talk to Baljeet, the cheap entry bell rings, and in dashes the young boy. This time, he's alone. He cuts directly behind Bobby's back and crouches to the ground. Bobby always turns around when the door opens, so I am surprised when Bobby stays facing me, without turning.

After a decade of working at Sunset, I know that the Pavlovian entry bell beats in Bobby's blood. Bobby and Baljeet have told me about the kids who steal chips and candy and even wine. So why is he still nodding politely, waiting for my next thought?

"Hey!" I say, and take a step to the right.

And now the boy stands up straight.

He looks me square in the eye.

"I left my basketball," he says. He sounds almost triumphant, proud that he remembered. In his rubberband arms he cradles a basketball as big as his chest. Then he turns and walks back out into the night.

NONFICTION

THE DOG PARK

By Susan Mann Flanders

Here's what it takes for me to walk Barney in January: Two pairs of socks, tights, corduroy pants, a turtleneck, a sweater, muffler, husband's long loden coat with hood, gloves and an old-fashioned black velvet muff, two plastic poop bags, electronic signal sender, ball. For Barney, electronic receiver collar, "gentle leader" collar, leash. Once all of this is in place, we head out into the freezing afternoon for at least an hour, Barney running eagerly ahead while I steel myself for the two-mile route, hoping for minimal winds.

We brought Barney home last January from deep southern Virginia where Elmo Londeree raises Brittany Spaniels as his family has done for generations. Our puppy was only 10 weeks old, romping through the high grass, fast and impossibly cute. He is brown and white, with freckles on his nose and nothing but a curly lock of hair instead of a tail. Brittanys are hunting dogs and need a lot of exercise, but they also make lovable, affectionate and loyal pets. I'd convinced Bill that a Brittany would be right for us. When we took Barney for shots, our vet eyed us, ages 80 and 70, and said, "You realize this is a very high-energy dog…"

Now, a year later, the dog park, actually two dog parks, are essential features of our life in Northwest Washington. The Livingston Road dog park is the morning scene. Reserved for dog walkers from 6:30-8:30 a.m., it offers a large fenced area where dogs run wild and free, tussling with each other as owners trudge the perimeter, talking and getting their own exercise—such a great multi-tasking daily routine! This is Bill's bailiwick, and he never misses a morning, even if it's five degrees. He has a band of friends, men and women, young and old, and they make their rounds, companionable without having to get too close.

Fort Reno Park is the afternoon venue, my routine, about a 20-minute walk each way. We start up the street and around the corner for a block until we reach one of the Alice Deal School playing fields. There Barney is released into blissful abandon and races off at top speed across the snow or through the brown leaves. A quick call brings him running all the way back to me, my way of establishing that we're in this together, then off he goes. We work our way around the school to the wooded hill in front. Here is squirrel territory, and running dog turns into hunting dog, standing stock still, watching for a glint of movement, a rustle in the leaves—and he's off! Head high, at full gallop in great sweeping circles, he covers the hillside, never catching a squirrel, following his primal instincts. I feel intense pleasure as I watch this little dog racing across the landscape, circling back to me and off again for another circuit.

We move on to what I think of as "the high plains," a huge, flat open area, sometimes in use as playing fields, often bare and windswept. Barney keeps running, back and forth, taunting an annoyed mockingbird who dive bombs him without effect. At last we reach the actual Fort Reno Park, a vast hillside with a broad plateau in the center where we dog owners gather with our pets—often as many as 15 dogs, between 4 and 5:30 p.m.—a little later in summer, earlier during the short days of winter.

We see Patrick, who lives next door, a black and white border collie, Barney's oldest friend. We see Artie, a copper-colored prancer, some rare duck-hunting breed, who brings a quick, edgy enthusiasm to all the best scuffles. Aphrodite, the queen, is there—majestic and aloof in her silver Alaskan Husky beauty, while her aging sister Zelda creeps around, almost blind, but loyal to owner Biff beyond reason. Huck, a giant black and white Standard Poodle bounds about, a good-willed long-legged puppy, always ready for a chase. And there is Chance, and Caspar, and Dakota, and Gumba, and Ruby Pearl, and Max—these are the names you get to know first; the owners are just appendages when you first start coming to the dog park.

But then, over time, you begin to know the people, and you become a part of the unique social grouping that a dog park is. These are not intimate friendships; often we don't know last names, or where each one lives exactly; often our talk is solely of dogs and weather, the two things we all have in common. But we see each other, many of us, every single day—for at least a half an hour! And so we do come to know what children we have, our spouses' names, the work we do or did. We review restaurants and movies avidly—again, safe territory, not too intimate, and we all live near the same places. We touch on politics and/or religion, but gingerly, not too sure where people are on these issues, and sometimes this leads to blunders— like the recent disparaging comments I made about George W. Bush to a woman whose husband was a top Bush advisor. I imagined her silence as stinging reproach as my faux pas dawned on me. Perhaps it's really better to stick to weather and dogs.

But then, we learn of someone's very bad diagnosis, or upcoming surgery, or loss of a dear one, and we realize we care about each other and have been drawn into each other's lives, unexpectedly, simply because we come to the park.

I walk up to the group, clustered among frolicking, grappling dogs.

"Hi Biff."

"Hello, Susan, how are you?"

"Fine—so how were the steaks Cathy cooked last night?"

"Fabulous—our sons devoured them—how was your dinner party?"

Meanwhile, another dog owner is glowering, hunched in indignation. As I sidle over, he tells me he can't stay—someone has lectured him because his dog was barking.

"But, that's what dogs do!" I respond. "Forget it." He laughs agreement, and the air is cleared. On different days, different people hold forth—we are all experts on something or other. Maggie is a savvy critic, cautioning us on various perils—to our gardens, our health, or on the general behavior of most people these days. She knows how to garden better than anyone and brings us all perfectly ripe tomatoes and lettuce in summer, huge sweet potatoes in the fall. She knows about raising dogs and cooking fresh food for them and the best gloves for the dog park and absolutely the best way to find bargains online and at Costco. And, I also learn she has some concerns about her grown son and family and is heading off to Boston to make sure all is well. And Janet is worried about her knee replacement next week, and lucky Carol has chosen this week of sub-freezing weather to lie on a beach in Nevis!

Edith's tall handsome son is applying to Harvard and is interested in drama. Elizabeth's grown daughter is visiting and hates movies, keeping Elizabeth from seeing all the Oscar nominees about which we vigorously compare opinions—"American Hustle," great—"Inside Llewyn Davis," hugely disappointing.

And Biff's son's classmate was one of the three Americans killed in the restaurant bombing in Kabul recently—a scathing shock to a whole community of young people who have grown up affluent and insulated from war's aching wounds. There has been a memorial service for the young friends only, full of tears and disbelief that this could happen to one of their own, one who went to school just blocks away, one who rowed crew and hung out in the family rec room.

Most days, three or four of us trudge towards home together in the fading freezing light, often with a pink and gold sunset behind us against the grey sky. The dogs continue their running and sniffing and playing; our own conversations wind down as we return to the rest of our lives. And so we weather the seasons of these parks and their canine and human communities. They are necessary for our dogs, perhaps even more so for us.

GENETIC IMPRINTS: THE COLOR OF MY DNA

By Patricia Aiken O'Neill

My father taught me the value of dressing for your audience. Not in so many words, but in modeling the language of communication and success. He was a natty dresser who intuitively knew that a certain mode of dress in a certain situation was akin to a calling card. His clothes modeled the language of success; people noticed him and remembered him.

When he returned to Washington after having first served in the Truman administration and then having carried the banner for the Democratic ticket for the U.S. Senate from Kansas, he donned the material of Washington politics: dress to impress, sometimes for power, or as punctuation to accompany a point that he intended to get across. His dress contributed to the elan that he projected. People took him seriously, and as a result, he had the luxury of not having to take himself too seriously. That comfort with himself made others around him comfortable. Today we call that "charisma," and his style was a part of the package.

He made sure that Mother's level of dress complemented his. But his clothes outlasted him, and when he died, Mother carried on what was to become a family tradition. She mixed the "true grit" of her Kansas beginnings with a mantle of Washington, DC sophistication that signaled a sense of belonging in her space, and in this place, her adopted home. She lived here for 60 years. Unlike my father, her dress exuded a different dialect of power, the power of graciousness and trust.

Her calling card was a fabulous purple coat that now hangs in my closet. It shelters her and she infuses it. With her scent still lingering, it speaks to me. I like to say that she "resides" in my closet and I intuitively know that her coat is her genetic imprint.

It's a coat that my father could have picked out for her. Mother and I shopped together downtown, covering F Street from Garfinckel's to "Woodies," both before and in the decades following the riots that rocked Washington in the aftermath of the tragedies of the late

1960s. It was a family tradition and brought us close to each other and to him—our missing link. This was a way for him to communicate through us.

Perhaps he was guiding us the day we found Mother's coat. It was a Washington power coat during a "Dynasty" era—shockingly purple, with a big bold stripe of black that ran geometrically down each side and extended on the sleeves across huge shoulder pads to its upright collar. We were not looking for anything special, but it was waiting for us.

Standing out on the sales rack, it called to us. We sensed immediately why it was on sale: It challenged the potential buyer to match its verve. Daddy's silent voice still retained power: He urged Mother to try it on. It both defined her and reinforced her elegance, her class and timeliness, all the qualities and color that she fashioned out of life. Each time she wore it, it became the screen that projected her as its star.

A decade later, following Mother's death, I reluctantly tasked myself with cleaning out her closet. Consigning so much that was familiar to me to either a charity or to longtime DC friends who wanted certain items as a reminder of her; I realized my own need for something to treasure, a memento of her. I fantasized that it would create a singular personal séance that would momentarily marry the present with the past. When I spotted her distinctive purple coat hanging in the closet, I felt that it was a talisman awaiting me. It could pass on my family's power to me.

Bereft, clearly missing its owner, it beckoned me like an orphan needing to be adopted. I approached it tentatively and hugged it, feeling her. I tried it on, knowing that I was no equal to its true mistress. But it nevertheless bestowed a kind of magic, enveloping me in her warmth as if she were with me once more. In one of the pockets was a handkerchief that had preserved an imprint of her distinctive pink lipstick. I drew it to my lips for a last lingering kiss, never wanting to let go.

Her scent permeated the coat, and for a fleeting moment in time, she was there with me. I remembered lightly applying perfume to each of her wrists as she was in the last stage of her illness. It awakened her senses. She instinctively knew what to do next: Ever so slowly, she had raised one arm to her face in a purposeful arc, suspending the march of her disease for a moment in time. It was gentle and slow and graceful. When her wrist barely caressed her nose, she had murmured softly, "Wonderful."

Now, facing me was this wonderful purple coat, inviting its potential new owner. It was my mother's residual, and I had to have it. I stole away, gingerly, with something that I knew was only meant to be hers, musing whether, like ancient Egyptians, perhaps this treasure belonged only to her.

But I soon banished those thoughts and wore it, trying to recapture my family heritage. It connected me to her and filled me with pleasure, but its title had not passed on to me, and I finally placed it in my closet, honoring its past—her past—and uncertain of its future. When I visit it now—my monument to my mother—it is sheltered and secure. It reminds me of "Joseph and the Amazing Technicolor Dreamcoat," a play we first saw at the Olney Theater: the story was that whoever wore the coat assumed its power. In the case of Mother's magnificent purple coat, the power passed to Mother only. Perhaps my charge was to find my own.

When I bought a purple coat from Rizik's, a woman's shop downtown on Connecticut Avenue close to where I worked, there was no obvious connection with Mother's coat. A decade had passed, and since I wasn't looking for it, I failed to consider how this new acquisition could connect me to the past and transport me to my future. It was swingy and bright and current. I picked the color from a palette that accompanied the sample. Vacillating between red and purple, I chose the latter because I was drawn to the color and thought the red was a little too obvious and bright. At that point, I didn't sense my purchase as a bridge from my mother to me.

But then, history began to repeat itself. Wearing my purple coat, a number of people commented on the color, the style—my style. Their compliments always pleased me, but I never considered anything beyond the pleasure it gave them to like it and me to wear it. Then one day, someone graciously executed a sweeping semi bow to me as we were exiting the Metro downtown, complimenting my purple coat and allowing me to proceed (and to precede him).

As I stepped forward, the wires connected: The power had transferred to me in my purple coat. My coat was the next generation of Mother's graciousness and style, of daddy's connection with others, and it had welcomed me to their world. It now belongs to me.

RECKONING

HOW THE NATION'S AIRPORT CAME TO BE CLOSED FOR 23 DAYS

By Tara Hamilton

On Tuesday, September 11, 2001, I was attending a conference sponsored by the Airports Council International in Montreal, Canada, along with 2,000 other airport managers and staff from every major airport in the U.S. and around the world.

We had just finished listening to the Canadian Minister of Transportation when the program was interrupted to announce an unthinkable event. A commercial jet had struck the World Trade Center in New York City. Within minutes, the jumbo screen in the convention hall showed a split screen of smoke billowing from one of the towers in New York and the Pentagon in Washington, DC.

Within three hours, the managers and staff of the Metropolitan Washington Airports Authority, who were attending the conference, were in rental cars heading across the border for home. We arrived at 1:30 a.m. We passed the Pentagon, which was still burning.

The next day, September 12, it was clear that airports around the country would remain closed. The Air Traffic Control system was still grounded. The FAA and Canadian air traffic controllers had successfully landed thousands of aircraft around the country and in Canada within hours of the attacks, and planes and people remained wherever they landed, like a cosmic game of Freeze.

The FAA was giving airports and airlines new security measures that had to be put in place before reopening. At airports across the country and at ours—Reagan National and Dulles International—airline managers were meeting with our airport staff to review these new security requirements and figure out how to implement them for the planned opening of the Air Traffic Control system the next day, September 13.

A command post was established at Reagan National in the conference room adjacent to the Airport Operations Office. This historic site once served as the private conference room for President Franklin D. Roosevelt, who had selected the site on which to build Reagan National and who oversaw its construction. The room had been lovingly restored four years earlier as part of a massive renovation and replacement program at the airport. We were "chiefs of war" sitting in that room, our own war of trying to make sense of what had happened, to understand what it meant for us as airport operators and to get back to work while answering the non-stop questions from the media on behalf of the public.

In the next five days we would speak to at least 55 news outlets on the issue of Reagan National and its reopening. But that was just the beginning.

On September 13, every airport in the country opened for business except two—Boston Logan and Reagan National.

Logan did open two days later, on September 15, but Reagan National remained closed for an unprecedented 23 days because of national security concerns. The official statement from the Federal Aviation Administration on September 13 said that because of its proximity to the Pentagon, Reagan National would be temporarily closed.

What would we tell the thousands of employees who worked at the airport? How would we answer questions from the public; the most difficult being, when will it open? These were questions that would remain for the next three weeks.

September 20, 2001, was the day we literally closed Reagan National Airport. We locked the doors—including the heavy metal ones at the end of the two pedestrian bridges that connected the terminal to the Metro system and the parking garages—turned down the ventilation system, switched off the lights, and sent the workers home.

As I walked through the massive concourse admiring its beauty, I could hear my own footsteps echoing along the hall. On a typical Friday at 4:00 p.m. the concourse would have been full of travelers coming in and out of shops, waiting in line for restaurant seats, and stopping by the Travelers Aid desk. That day, it was empty. I looked to my left out of the expansive window wall at the empty ramp areas. Not a plane to be seen. Fifty-one planes had been left at the gates when the terminal was evacuated on September 11, and the airlines had flown them all out days ago.

Just three days before, we held a major press conference in this hall with the Governor of Virginia calling for the opening of the airport, followed by two days of major demonstrations of support for opening the airport by the elected officials in Congress, local jurisdictions, and the business community. The airport workers had held a rally just hours before, calling on the President to put them back to work, as he had urged the country to go back to work.

Now, I walked through the airport terminal that we had introduced to the public just five years before. The "New National" was a great reconstruction project that made a truly fitting entry to the nation's capital.

I took in the beauty of the terminal and its wonderful artwork. I looked at it again, only more closely than I had every other day. How could this building close? How could my hometown, my city's airport, be no more? How could the place that thousands of people came to work in every day, and thousands more came to board aircraft, be no more?

I couldn't and wouldn't believe it.

By Thursday, September 27, Reagan National was the only airport in the country not yet open, and it appeared that the decision was with the National Security Council and the Secret Service.

As the days continued, there was growing support in the Washington region to open Reagan National. The arguments were predominantly economic, since the airport not only employed thousands of people but also was a huge generator of revenue for the region.

The biggest frustration for me about the continued closing was the obvious lack of logic. The proximity of Reagan National to the Pentagon and other government buildings didn't make the airport a security risk. The security issue should have been about who was flying the aircraft, not where the airport was located.

After more days of high-level meetings of the government agencies involved in national security and aviation, President George W. Bush decided to make an announcement on October 2.

At 10:45 a.m., the motorcade rolled onto the ramp area at Reagan National near Terminal B and people started clapping. The gathered employees wildly cheered President Bush when he announced that Reagan National would open on Thursday, October 4.

Our airport community was happy, but faced with an amazing turnaround in a short period. There were no complaints. The local airline station managers were people who got things done. On a good day, in what used to be normal times, they put up with every conceivable problem that could be imagined in operating hundreds of flights, managing employees, and serving the public. Those last three weeks had been painful for them. They had to send their employees home and wonder about their own futures. But that day, it was all about doing the job.

On Thursday, October 4, we programmed "Welcome Back" and "We're Back in Business" onto our electronic message boards at the airport entrances and on our displays in the terminal.

It began that day with 190 total flights allowed during the first three weeks, increasing to 450 flights over the next 45 days. Before September 11, our usual day saw 700 or more scheduled flights.

The closing of Reagan National had brought the region's elected leaders, business community, and the general public together as never before. The nation's—and DC's—airport was finally open again.

This is one of thousands of stories we can all tell about 9/11/01— the day that changed our lives and our country's sense of security. This is the story of an airport and its importance to the people and community it serves.

DISTRICT LINES

UNDER THE 14TH STREET BRIDGE

By Renee Gherity

Jet fuel particles misted psychedelic,
sky to water, as he filled the tanks,
stocked the galley with cold cuts and fruit,
and the ice chests with liquor and beer.

His family, friends, and even ex-lovers,
joined him for one last trip to Smoot's Cove
before he and his new bride moved to California
where he slumped over his piano
and died.

They all gathered by the river,
no funeral prayers, no eulogies or hymns
just the tin sound of his a cappella group
singing, "*What a Wonderful World*,"
from a small cassette player
as his daughters opened the urn,
cast him across the river
to mix with rainbow oil
and the Potomac flowing to Smoot's Cove.

:: DISTRICT LINES ::

TO-DO LIST

By Erin Page

Laurie killed her ficus tree a week after moving into her new home. The little tree had survived more than 15 years and countless moves. On the first day in its new place by the front window of the townhouse, the leaves began to shiver. Laurie thought the tree had found a draft. By the third day, however, the leaves were falling steadily, and by the seventh, the tree was as bare as a broken umbrella.

"Maybe it's getting used to the climate," Evan said.

"Maybe we'll all die if we can't get the air conditioning fixed," Laurie responded.

Evan picked up the tree—pot, leaves, and all—and took it out to the trash.

Cool, Laurie said to herself, watching Evan inexpertly wield the ungainly tree skeleton and the dented DC city trashcan lid. We'll talk again in a week when I have something else to complain about.

"It's going to be a long six months if you're already not speaking," Bridget told her over the phone. She stretched out the word "long" for about three seconds, but Laurie couldn't hear the caution in her friend's voice. Bridget was from New Jersey and added an extra syllable to the word for a hard guh sound at the end. It was never not hilarious.

"You're not wronguh," said Laurie.

"Don't be that person," Bridget warned. "Give him a nice memory to take with him for when he ships out. How do you think he feels if every time he comes home you give him grief?"

Laurie had to wonder then if her old college roommate and her mother were sitting together in Bridget's living room. She could imagine her mother scratching out notes for Bridget to paraphrase. "Husband = HERO" one would say. I warned her to cut this shit out when she was younger.

On Saturday, Evan took the kids to the National Zoo. Laurie walked around each room in the new house and made a to-do list, which eventually covered three pages of a legal pad. She read through the whole list again over her morning coffee. She was pretty sure she could taste a difference in the water. She picked an item on the third page and started there.

They didn't spend long in any house or city because Evan was a Marine, and they traveled with him regularly as he was shifted from post to post. Laurie's favorite home had been in Buffalo because that was where her grandmother lived. Polly lived alone and Laurie visited her at least once a week, bringing Rosalind in diapers. Rosalind had liked poking at the photographs and walls of Polly's small house, and she would sit in rapt attention when Polly would tell her charming half-truths about the family members smiling out of each of the frames. When Polly passed three years ago, Laurie collected all of her photographs. She kept them displayed in the exact order as her grandmother had in every house they moved into.

She pulled out a single frame from its packing box and found herself frozen in place. It was one she rarely looked at, perhaps because it was hung at waist-level in her wall diagram, but more likely because the people in it were so small. The photo showed more of a stone church than it did the couple exiting through the front doors, hand-in-hand, just-married. The groom wore a Marine dress uniform. Bright sunlight glinted off of his slicked dark hair as he turned to look at his bride. The young woman was squinting happily at him, wearing a full veil that poured off of the back of her head and trailed all the way to meet the train of her gown.

Rosalind liked that photo of Laurie's parents because, she always said, "Grandma looks like a princess, and Grandpa looks like a prince." Rosalind never said that about Laurie; there weren't any pictures of Laurie's wedding.

Laurie and Evan were married in the courthouse in their college town. The only witnesses were the city hall officials and two student reporters. They had graduated only a month before and were headed directly from Evan's student apartment to boot camp. Evan would be at boot camp, anyway, and Laurie would be renting a room not far away. They wore the only clothes they hadn't packed into their suitcases. If there had been a camera, she would have been smiling for it.

Laurie had wanted to marry Evan since the night they met during their sophomore year. He was alternately chugging a coffee and furiously typing on a laptop at the best-lit table in the bar. Laurie was with two of her friends who had both just broken up with their boyfriends and were more interested in rehashing their anger than chatting up any fresh faces, so Laurie had wandered the bar by herself before sitting down across from Evan.

It took a full minute before Evan noticed her presence. It was long enough for her to fall in love with the way the harsh lighting bounced around his curly hair. When he finally noticed her, he grinned and offered to buy her a cup of coffee.

"Let me guess," she said after taking him up on the offer. "Mormon?"

"Guess again," he responded, his grin broadening.

"Teetotaler," she tried. "Former alcoholic. You might look like you're 15, but you're actually 47, twice divorced and not allowed to drive. You're on the straight and narrow hoping to win back your ex."

"Wow, you're bad at this," he said with a laugh. "No, none of the above. Actually I drink quite a bit. I've been drinking for most of the past month, however, I've got a term paper due tomorrow, so..."

"So you'd like me to stop bothering you."

"No. Not at all," he said. He had stopped smiling and was looking at her rather like he had been looking at his computer a few minutes before; curiously, a bit frantically, but with an underlying confidence that he was going to figure things out. "I always work better if there is a pretty girl hanging around to inspire me."

The coffee arrived then with a little tub of creamers and sweeteners. "My turn to guess," said Evan. "Three packets of sweetener, no cream."

He was right. He was always incredibly good at figuring her out, except for one thing.

Laurie put the framed photo of her parents back in the box. As she stepped back, she noticed a little pile of ants in the corner of the living room. She was surprised how relieved she was to find another task to accomplish before tacking the photo back up again. She didn't add the task to her list. She never really finished the list, anyway.

★ ★ ★

The kids had registration day at their new school that week. Rosalind, who was nine, could be relied upon to at least carry the paperwork that Laurie had completed, but she would still need shepherding throughout the morning to the photo session, meeting with the school counselor, and visiting her classroom. Jamie, who was three, needed his paperwork and potentially his person carried for him.

When the kids were reasonably well-dressed, combed, fed, and occupied with new little backpacks, Laurie found Evan in the living room. He was wearing his oldest pair of flip-flops and was working his way through the latest "Grand Theft Auto," on silent.

"Are you almost ready to go?" she asked.

Evan stared hard at the television screen with his mouth slightly open. Laurie had always thought he had a profile like a Roman emperor, so she was at least afforded that view while she awaited his response.

"Are you?"

"Am I what?" he asked. "Let me pause."

When he paused the game a black shadow veiled the screen, though you could still see the frozen avatar driving into a San Andres alleyway filled with armed men. Evan always said he would never play "Call of Duty" because war wasn't a game, but he seemed perfectly fine waging gang warfare on a regular basis.

"I thought we were going to registration day with the kids together," she said.

Evan sighed. "We were going to, but then I found out I had the extra half of the week on leave so I wasn't going to. Do you remember?"

She remembered because Evan had found out yesterday, and because he had similarly used the phrase "on leave," which irritated her. His superior's flight had been canceled and he couldn't get another departure from Erbil for three more days; he had given Evan the word to enjoy the extra time. Evan had been relieved because he was nervous about his first day at his new post. He was also nervous about driving all the way through downtown Washington and out into Arlington to the Pentagon, though he had refused Laurie's offers to practice the route. He insisted her presence would make him even more nervous. He had said all this, but nothing about skipping registration day.

"I have those days off, too," she said. "I'm still going."

"You have the whole week off and next," Evan said. "So it's

less of a burden on your time, is what I was thinking."

Laurie could hear the kids' attention to their new school supplies beginning to wane as the sounds from the foyer grew louder. "It would be better if we could both go so that one of us could go with each kid and meet their teachers, you know, introduce ourselves. I don't want Rosalind to have to go around by herself..."

"She's nine, she can totally go around by herself. She'll probably like it better without her parents following her around."

"Can't you just come, please?"

Evan gestured to the shirt and shorts he had slept in and was still wearing.

A soft, splattering crash came from the front of the townhouse. Her mind leapt to the ficus tree before she remembered.

She found herself waiting anxiously for Evan to return when he finally went out on his first day of work. Jamie, who only went to preschool for the mornings, was napping before dinner, and Rosalind was at soccer practice after school, so Laurie surprised herself by sitting at their breakfast counter, perched on a stool, alternately checking her phone and staring into the middle distance outside their small new kitchen.

It was her most dreaded moment any time they moved, the aimless waiting. Sometimes she already had a new job by now and sometimes she didn't, but in either case there was always a time when they first moved to a new city and she found a nameless fear while she waited for Evan to come home. Evan was not posted abroad anymore. He was older now and had kids, and he had served twice in Iraq; his career track was secured by ever-more-distinguished posts stateside. It wasn't fear borne out of concern for his safety. It was something else, but it was strong enough to freeze her in place. The fear increased as each minute ticked by, and she knew it, and yet she held her ground in her futility. She was a party to the fear. She gave in and felt it in full each time.

The cell phone buzzed in her hand. She jumped in her seat. Her thumb automatically slid across the screen to answer even as she recognized that it wasn't Evan calling her at all, but rather a number she didn't recognize.

"This is Laurie Bendel speaking. May I ask who is calling, please?" Funny how she slipped into the old way she used to answer phones as a kid. "Sorry, I mean Laurie Marx. Sorry."

"Hi, Mrs. Marx. I am calling about the order you placed with Sheldon & Partridge Furniture?"

Item No. 18 on her list. Maybe this afternoon wouldn't be a total loss. "Yes?"

"I am sorry it has taken us a few days to follow up on your order, but unfortunately, we can't ship outside of the United States."

"What? Wait." She put her hand to her temple, as though she could physically jolt her brain into a fully functioning mode. "This is, um, this is for the order... for the sofa set. Online. Where did I say I wanted it shipped?"

"You put down the District of Columbia. Unfortunately, we can't ship the larger pieces outside of the United States per the policy listed on our website. Unless you have a different address where we can ship them we will unfortunately have to cancel the order..."

Laurie put the phone back down on the counter and tapped it to hang up.

She stared at her phone for a long while because suddenly her fear had a name, and it was It Wasn't Supposed to Be Like This But I Let It Happen. Its last name was Because I'm Not As Smart As I Thought I Was.

During their senior year of college, Evan got an itch. Not to see other women, of course; they were happier together than anyone else they knew. He had been studying chemical engineering throughout his undergraduate course, when suddenly he decided he wanted to join the armed forces. He had never been interested in ROTC, had no friends who were planning to sign up, and no enlisted family members, but suddenly and without ever fully explaining, he gave up everything he had been planning and prepared to sign up the day after graduation. He picked the Marines because, he said, "They're the most intense. It feels right," and just as intensely, it changed his entire life.

His friends and family were worried at this sudden upending of his life. His mother even begged him to get a scan to see if he had a brain tumor. But from the day he began announcing his decision to everyone he met to the day he put on his uniform and headed to boot camp, he never wavered in his reasoning.

"I just need to do this. I need to fight for my country." That is how he put it to Laurie on the first day. They both had tears in their eyes. "Please come with me. There is nothing else I would want more than for you to come with me. But I'll understand if you don't."

There were tears in her eyes but they didn't fall. She was quiet for a long time. She said, "I will."

From that day on, she was a military wife. They got married early, had kids early, and traveled early and often, just like all the other military families. Just like that, with two words, she was agreeing to the life she had always sworn she would stop leading.

She had been an army brat growing up, living on and off bases while her father served and her mother waited. It was a Thing That Required Explaining at all times, in classes, when meeting new friends, and when saying good-bye to old friends. When she was 12 and they lived in San Antonio, she had a friend who had a fake leg. She eventually grew apart from her friend because every time they were together she couldn't stop thinking, "You never have to explain that. People accept it. No one looks for a better answer from you." She felt bad thinking it, and she felt bad for abandoning her friend. But they moved soon enough and eventually she forgot to feel bad. She always seethed with the desire to leave everything behind. College was her first, and ultimately last, chance to stop explaining herself.

In that moment that she agreed to Evan, though, she agreed to everything that came with it. When she was angry with him for inconveniences that she felt were foisted upon her life, she was equally angry with herself, because she had done an equal amount of foisting. Evan had never been anything less than completely honest with himself and everyone else. It didn't bother him that he was living the most patriotic life he could lead and the people he had risked his life to protect didn't know where Washington, DC was. All of it, the moving, the kid-uprooting, and the lack of sense that she felt for his duty bothered her.

Sitting at the counter, however, because her sofa was never going to arrive, Laurie gave another name to her fear, and it was Because I Can't Face My Own Answers. Evan had never given her a satisfactory answer for changing his life's work, but it wasn't really what she needed. She kept avoiding having to explain herself because she wasn't sure of the real answer. She had been so focused on not becoming a Military Wife that she lived in the negative space. She didn't know what it is she wanted to do, how else she should have done things. She knew that much because she had said, "I will," because there had been no other answer. If she could keep busy with her tasks, keep setting up house and tearing it down as necessary, it was enough. It was enough to get her moving and tamp down the fear. A life of days with tasks checked off could be enough to speak for itself.

The living room of the new townhouse in downtown DC was starkly empty without couches to fill it. A few ants still circled the traps she had laid. Jamie should be waking up from his nap soon, or else he would be difficult to put down for the night.

She would hang up all the photographs first.

MOTORCADE
By Rob Winters

Sirens. Lights. Harleys. Roadblocks.
"Black on black" SUVs pass.
Tourists stop. Locals walk on.

RUSH HOUR

By Gina Brown

Construction again. Why is construction allowed during rush hour? Doesn't the city know people are trying to get to work? We can't maneuver with one lane. We need more lanes. Why aren't there more lanes?

Why are you driving down this street if you don't have a kid to drop off at school? There are lots of other streets. The bell is going to ring in five minutes. The kids need to be in school. Your car, without kids in it, is in my way. Tomorrow, take another street. Where are you going, anyway?

When did a bicycle become a vehicle? Why is there a lane, taking up half of my driving lane, earmarked for bicycles? Bicycles are for sport. Sport doesn't happen during rush hour. Sport happens on the weekend. It's Wednesday at 8:10 a.m.

Why do I have to play chicken every morning on Connecticut Avenue? We all know four lanes are open going south until 9:30 a.m. You have DC plates. You are not a visitor. Why are you going north anyway? We're all going south. Why can't all six lanes go south in the morning? Where are you going?

What are they building in Van Ness? Will it ever actually get constructed? Do we need more luxury condos? Why can't we just have a new, regular building go up? Why does everything have to be more luxurious? What's wrong with regular?

Why are there crosswalks in the middle of the street? Crosswalks should require a traffic light. I feel guilty if I don't stop to let you cross, but where are you going? I'm going to work. Are you going to work? Are you under time constraints?

How do you have time to jog in the morning? It's 8:45 a.m. Why aren't you in a car beeping at a bicyclist? Why is your morning time more leisurely than mine? I wonder where you work. I wonder if you work.

Why can't you catch that cab in an alley? I was driving in that right lane and now I have to stop. The light is green—please hurry up and close the door. Why did you catch the cab going east if you needed to go west? Now he has to make a U-turn. You know it's rush hour, right? Where are you going?

Is it trash collection day again? Just like construction, this should not be allowed during rush hour. I can't get around you. Please close the back of the truck. That trash smell is coming through my air vents. Gosh, you could have at least put the trash can to the side of the driveway. Later, the homeowners will just have to block traffic, while they hazard, and move the trash can out of their driveway.

How hard could it be to fill a pothole? Pour some asphalt in the hole at midnight. Let it sit. Done. And no impact to rush hour.

Why didn't you speed up to go through that light? It was yellow. Not red. Today is not Sunday. Everybody speeds around the circle. It's Dupont Circle. The name means "speed." Yes, I'm glaring at you in your rearview mirror. Where are you going?

A left turn? We don't turn left here during rush hour. It's Massachusetts Avenue. We only go straight on Massachusetts Avenue. Yes, you can turn left, but not at this hour. It holds all of us up. And we can't be held up. Now I have to sit in front of the Embassy of Australia again. Gosh, that's a big embassy. The embassy is bigger than the country itself. What kind of business are we doing with Australia?

Is that a DC cop? Are you following me? Why are your lights flickering? Are you asking me to pull over? I stopped at Scott Circle. I can describe every person that walked into the Embassy of Australia. Ok, I'm pulled over. Wait, why are you driving past me? You're not even on pursuit? Then why are your lights on?

Where are YOU going?

FICTION

JERICHO ROAD

By Fiona J. Mackintosh

The first time I see them he's beating her head against the roof of his car.

I'm in the kitchen making coffee when I first hear it, a rhythmic thud-thud-thud. I'm taking a break, the long transcription two-thirds done, still in my pajama bottoms and a sweatshirt with a hole in the elbow. The percolator bubbles and spits. Waiting, I drift into the living room and stroke the cat, who's stretched out on the sofa like a flying monkey. I hear it again, the thud-thud-thud, and another noise I can't place, a kind of keening. I look out the bay window between the security bars, and half a block up Constitution, there they are.

I'm out in the street before I know it, barefoot on the hot pavement.

"Hey!"

The man, tall, slim, well-dressed, turns his head and glares. He has her face pressed sideways against the metal roof.

"Let her go!"

I hesitate just outside my gate. What if he has a gun?

"I'm calling the cops. Right now!"

Then I realize my phone is inside.

"Ma'am, run over here. Come here to my house. Get away from him."

His fist in her hair is twisted so tight her eyes are slanted.

"Not your business, lady."

He doesn't shout but his voice carries. The woman gestures at me, waving me away. Am I making things worse? Again her head smacks against metal, hard.

A cop car—no siren—swings up 10th and pulls up to the curb. Someone must have called. The man lets go of the woman's hair but grabs her wrist.

Jeri from across the street hurries over.

"You okay, hon?"

"Did you see that? In broad daylight! I tried to get her to come

DISTRICT LINES

to me but she wouldn't. I didn't know what else to do."

"Sweetie, that kind of woman won't listen to reason."

DC's finest get out like they have all the time in the world. One pats the man down and then walks him to the corner. The man's hands are raised, palms out, like he's saying, "It's all good, officer. Just a misunderstanding." The other cop, his notebook out, talks to the woman.

She bends low over her crossed arms and shakes her head at every question he asks.

The officers confer, then drift towards their cruiser.

"She's sending them away? I don't believe it."

The woman moves round to the passenger side of the car, smoothing her hair. The morning sun spotlights the place on the roof where her face was pressed, filmed with skin cells and sweat and DNA. As she gets in the car, she shoots me a look under her brows, hostile, strangely triumphant.

"Oh my god, what is her problem? He could have killed her."

Jeri shakes her head.

"It's a sickness, hon. They can't help themselves. I pray they don't have children. They're the ones I feel bad for."

The next time I see them they're sitting at a bar, wound around each other, her long shiny legs rubbing up against his.

It's a Friday night at Rumors downtown. I'm with a bunch of people from a client company, a happy hour that turned into a night out. I lean way back in my chair to get a better look. It's definitely them. He caresses a long curl of her hair like he's fingering expensive fabric. She's laughing with him, fitted into the curve of his body.

Between the churning dancers, I watch them. When she slides off her bar stool, I follow her into the ladies' room. In my stall, I scribble my phone number on the back of a CVS receipt I've found in my wallet. Just 10 digits and two initials—nothing else. When I hear her flush, I come out and lean into the mirror right next to her. Her eyes flick to my face and then away. No sign of recognition.

A cluster of girls bursts into the ladies' room, shrieking and slamming stall doors, shouting and laughing to each other over the partitions. I have the note in my hand. She presses her lips together to set her gloss. As she pushes back a curve of hair, there's a greenish half-moon over her brow, and again I see the man's hands in her hair, the white knuckling of his grip, and the look on her face as she got into the car. A look that said, "Back off, bitch. You know nothing."

I push the note back into my purse and reach in front of her—"Excuse me"—to pump the soap dispenser. As I'm waving my hands beneath the faucet sensor, she turns on her high heels and leaves the bathroom. The laughing girls crowd up to the sinks, a miasma of perfume, hair spray, and alcohol breath. I look into my eyes in the mirror and wring my hands under the sudden rush of water.

NONFICTION

FAREWELL TO THE FIGHT

By Matt Finkelstein

For me, working in politics was more like "The Office" than "The West Wing" or "House of Cards." It happened haphazardly, if not quite randomly, as I grappled with the reality of growing up. Having tried and failed to break into publishing in New York, I was still looking for my first real job. I hoped to find a career that would offer meaning and, I admit, a certain level of prestige. More than anything else, I desperately wanted to matter. I believed that I could make a difference and hoped that I would, but the main reason I started working in politics is that politics would have me. Then I got sucked in by the idea of politics, by the illusion of influence, by the promise that I was always one step away from having an impact. But as I rose through the ranks, my spirit slowly sank. Yes, there were good days, but they were outnumbered by the weeks wasted on Twitter, waiting for something to happen. Most of the time, it was just a job like any other—one that wore me down, made me question my self-worth, and left me longing for more. Finally, I quit because I decided that politics, which embraced me when nobody else would, had no use for the person I wanted to be.

I arrived in the nation's capital in January 2009, almost two years after I graduated from college and two months shy of my 24th birthday, to start working at a liberal nonprofit. On the morning before my first day, I woke up at 6:15 a.m., showered, and walked a mile down Connecticut Avenue to the Metro in the dark. A few stops later, I came up the escalator and felt a blast of cold wind across my face as I surveyed the unfamiliar intersection. I didn't stop at the coffee shop on the corner because caffeine was not yet a daily necessity. Just before 7:30, I watched a young woman with wet hair and a bursting backpack enter the building looking like a weary student on the morning of a final exam. This was a dry run; the next day I

DISTRICT LINES

would be walking in behind her. I would stay inside, so to speak, for the next five years.

My first boss was a former adviser to a leader in the Senate, but he looked more like a mad scientist, or perhaps an overgrown middle schooler. He had dark, curly hair that formed perfect right angles on his big block of a head. At 30 years old, he was baby-faced with a look in his eyes that fluctuated between wonderment and impatience. I don't remember how he was dressed on the day we met—the day he hired me—but I imagine him wearing an untucked collared shirt, wrinkled khakis, and a pair of New Balances or Nike Dunks. That afternoon, he leaned back in his chair and rested his feet on the conference room table. Our conversation was brief. Then he led me to an empty cubicle, past a handful of twentysomethings sporting massive headphones and staring at monitors, and handed me a printout of a press release.

"Refute this. I'll be back in 25 or 30 minutes," he said and walked away briskly.

When he returned, he glanced over my shoulder for no more than a few seconds and clicked the red "X" in the top right corner of the screen. He didn't bother to save the document on which I had staked my entire future.

"The job is yours if you want it," he said. "You can think about it for a few days and let me know."

"I'm ready to accept now," I answered.

In the early days, there were just a half-dozen of us in a small room that had recently served as a storage closet. As I browsed the blogosphere for political fodder, my boss was usually pacing or re-clining in his desk chair, eyes darting around his computer screen like a predator looking for an opportunity to pounce. When he located his target, he would yell something like "I'm going to poop on your head!" and start typing frantically, pumping out a withering blog post in a matter of minutes. I always laughed, not appreciating that reality wasn't so far from the joke.

I didn't appreciate it, I think, because I so badly wanted to believe that I had made it. The road to that first job spanned two cities, three internships, and more false starts than I can count. It peaked with a stint at *Esquire*, the home of so much timeless writing, where I mainly conducted research for the sex column—by which I mean cold-calling doctors and sex therapists and adult film actresses with humiliating questions. Then came unemployment, rejection, and the descent into depression. Although my parents were paying my rent in New York, I got a small taste of how joblessness can make a person desperate for distraction. In my case, I became obsessed with the presidential election between Barack Obama and John McCain. In the fall of 2008, my daily routine was consistent: sleep late, check the job listings, and scour the Internet for news about the campaign. I needed to see the latest polls in the battleground states. I had to know who had said what and why to be outraged. I even started watching cable news. Meanwhile, when I visited my girlfriend in Washington, I would stroll around the city and marvel at its sense of peace.

For several months after I moved, I rarely strayed from the stretch of the Red Line that runs from downtown to the upscale Maryland suburb of Bethesda, with the sleepy Van Ness neighborhood where I lived sandwiched in between. I still remember walking from the office near Dupont Circle to the U Street Corridor, an area in the midst of gentrification, to play basketball and feeling like I was in another city altogether. Before long, we traded our converted-closet bullpen for a shiny new office in Chinatown, expanding my horizons by a couple of Metro stops. And when I got married in 2011, my wife and I bought a condo barely a block from the basketball court where I used to play. As the neighborhood blossomed with trendy restaurants and luxury apartment buildings, it became a magnet for the city's successful young professionals—a crowd that somehow had come to include me.

But even then, I felt like I was faking it. As I climbed the professional ladder, I viewed each step as temporary, a means of establishing credibility, a springboard that would finally launch me toward something better. I didn't understand the people who bounced from campaign to campaign, or organization to organization, chasing news cycles and making partisan politics into an actual career. It took a long time to accept that I had become one of them. But when people asked what I did for a living, I finally replaced "I'm a writer" with "I work at a political organization" or "It's kind of hard to explain."

It really was hard to explain, at least in a way that didn't make me feel ridiculous. My title changed—Washington is full of deputies of this and directors of that—but the work remained essentially the same: I searched wherever I could for political ammunition and attacked the other side online. I monitored cable news, floor speeches, press releases, newspaper columns, and Twitter feeds, hunting for gaffes and lies. I played gotcha and called bullshit. There were times when it was fun. On my best days, I influenced a national news story or inspired a segment on "The Daily Show." More often than not, however, I was shouting into television screens and pounding on my keyboard to make points that would only reach a small number of political obsessives, who already agreed with me or didn't.

We often hear about a "campaign of ideas," but I came to believe that our public discourse makes that impossible. The problem is that politics is a long-term game in which the players compete to win short-term contests—elections, the news cycle, and, in the age of Twitter, the moment. And while you can't win a substantive argument in 140 characters or a sound bite, you can mock opponents or pander to a crowd. But there is little to gain from nuance or honest engagement with conflicting ideas, so we rarely bother attempting to change minds. The more immersed I became in politics, the less intelligent, creative, and interesting I felt. I hated going out to dinner and hearing people a table over having the same conversations I had all day. I hated talking to friends in other cities and struggling to think of anything else to bring up. The cynicism took hold gradually, but it was a powerful, paralyzing force.

In June 2012, as campaign season was heating up, my father-in-law passed away. He was only 59 years old, but he didn't waste the time he got. Based on the overwhelming response to his death—from the large family he treasured, the legal clients he represented, and even the lawmakers who represented him in Congress—it was obvious that he mattered to the world around him. The heartbreaking reminder of a life lived with purpose made me realize that I was adrift. I started telling people close to me that I was ready to move on; I would stay through Election Day and then figure it out. But when I went back to work, the daily routine took over again. On the night of the election, we had a party at the office, and after the networks called Ohio, a bunch of us went to the roof and drank an expensive bottle of scotch. We got to stay home for the rest of the week, but once the election hangover wore off, I had to tell half my team they were losing their jobs. The campaign was over, and I was still there.

One morning the next spring, I awoke to an unwelcome work email, walked out of my apartment, and kicked a tree in frustration. I could almost wrap my fingers around its flimsy white trunk, which rose maybe 15 feet into the air from a dirt patch on the sidewalk, but the force of impact still hurt the ball of my foot. Then I stopped for coffee and dragged myself to the office, limping slightly and dreading the day ahead. That's when I knew, once and for all, that I had to leave. But leaving was easier said than done. In 2013, it was like I was 23 all over again—résumés went unanswered, emails were blown off, interviews led nowhere. In some ways, it was worse. In 2008, I was inexperienced and untested, but my options were almost limitless. Now, I had experience, but it was the wrong experience. I wanted to leave politics behind, but I couldn't imagine other possibilities. I was stuck.

Later that summer, my wife and I had a fight. We were never a couple that fought, but we got into a stupid argument one night—I thought she was being unfair, I said something mean, and she got mad—and I started to cry. It was a hard, violent cry from somewhere deep inside, a cry like I never remember crying before, a cry totally out of proportion to the pettiness that provoked it. I cried for a few minutes until I stopped, began trembling, and got really cold. My wife wrapped me in a blanket, but then I was too hot. I told her I was sorry, and then I started hyperventilating, which went on for several more minutes. At one point, for no apparent reason, I laughed hysterically for maybe 20 seconds. After taking a lot of deep breaths and finally calming down, I felt tingling in my hands and an impulse to keep my eyes wide open. When it was over, I was exhausted and felt something like peace.

I finally accepted that it wasn't politics that was holding me back. The problem was me. If I wanted something more, I had to take action, and maybe even a risk. So I turned down another job in politics and gave notice. For the first time in years, I didn't have a plan—but I was finally free. My last day was exactly two years after my father-in-law passed away. Instead of celebrating, I went to synagogue with my wife and said the Mourner's Kaddish for her dad. That was almost a year ago now, but it feels like much longer. Although we still live in Washington, it's hard to remember the days dominated by talking points and tweets, and my ears don't perk up anymore when I hear a politician's name at dinner. Every now and then, I see a political story trending online, shake my head, and try to imagine what the old me would have thought. Then I close the browser and go back to work. I have a good job, I'm writing, and I'm happy. I don't know if I'm making a difference, not in the way that I used to think I would, but I have a new definition of what it means to matter.

AFTERNOON AT ARLINGTON CEMETERY

By Karen Sagstetter

Our dad, old veteran,
cornball talker,
stops strangers on street corners:
great Collie you have there, your kids
sure are high, wide and handsome.
People love it, or they twitch,
and check their watches.

He refuses to fritter money
on funerals, insists on the cheapest, so
his fresh ashes are solemnly interred
by a grateful nation (honor guard,
bugles) in a green plastic box.
He would've laughed about that.
He would've liked the sunny columbarium,
the army private from Colorado
who in 1945 marched into Buchenwald.

TUESDAYS AT WALTER REED

By Bob Johnson

Captain Stevens*, an Army nurse, usually got to class first. Of course all he had to do was walk downstairs from his office to the basement of the General Creighton W. Abrams barracks at the Walter Reed Army Medical Center. I, an Army Reserve infantry major, usually got there second, taking the DC Metro's Yellow line from the Pentagon, then the red to Takoma, and finally, a short walk to the campus on Georgia Avenue. Colonel Brown, an Army Reserve doctor, typically was next, walking over from his quarters at Walter Reed's Malone House. Captain Davis, an Army chaplain, usually was late.

Others came in and out of the program, but the chaplain, the nurse, and the doctor were the core of the group that participated in the Walter Reed Wounded Warrior Writing Program, a writing support group I started in the winter of 2010. The program provided a safe environment for recently injured service members and their caregivers to use writing as therapy to deal with their newly acquired demons. We met every Tuesday from 6 to 8 p.m. for more than a year.

Today, Captain Stevens was the first to read—he always wanted to go first. He continued with his story about Fatima, a seriously burned Iraqi girl he had treated when she was brought to the Army field hospital in Baghdad. She had just reached puberty, the first time she could fast for Ramadan, and was looking forward to participating in the ritual when her house was fire bombed, killing her mother and one brother. Initially it wasn't clear whether the attack involved friendly fire, which was why she was treated at an Army field hospital in the first place. When it was determined that the attack was not by coalition forces, the hospital prepared to release Fatima to her family, classifying her as expectant, medical language for "expected to die." While her injuries were serious, they were survivable and deemed expectant only because Iraq didn't have a burn hospital capable of treating her. When Captain Stevens found this out, he interceded and saved her life.

* *Stevens, Brown, and Davis are fictitious names, changed for confidentiality*

Fatima's emotions about her duties to Islam were new to Stevens, but he knew Fatima needed to eat and drink to recover from her wounds. Still, she wanted to fast and refused treatment. As he held her hand, a thought came to Stevens—he would take over the ritual for her!

"Fatima," he blurted out, "I will fast for you!"

First puzzled, Fatima asked her father if that was possible and then, after a nod, smiled and accepted Stevens' offer. She drank some water and soon fell asleep. People in the hospital room looked at Stevens and wondered if he was nuts. He wasn't. Now on the hook for not eating or drinking during daylight hours for a month, Stevens kept that promise. With that, Stevens finished reading.

Colonel Brown, a Harvard-educated Army surgeon who was a patient at Walter Reed, was up next. Colonel Brown suffered from encephalitis, an illness he felt was caused by the anthrax vaccinations soldiers were required to take prior to and during deployment. He wrote his stories in cursive on single-spaced lined paper. His doctor told him that the class would be therapeutic counter to the ravages of the disease inside his head that affected his short-term memory. Colonel Brown's favorite saying was, "You can't make this shit up," as he wrote about the absurdities that result from the collision of military bureaucracy and war.

While Colonel Brown often wrote about his disease, today his story was about being threatened with a court martial for trying to save a grievously wounded soldier. The soldier had already lost his legs and could not be stabilized for a lifesaving evacuation flight to Landstuhl Regional Medical Center in Germany. The week before, a colleague in the states, a fellow thoracic surgeon, had mailed what Colonel Brown called "the device," an unapproved experimental external breathing apparatus. Colonel Brown had collaborated on developing the device with his colleague before Brown deployed to Iraq and tried using it on the wounded soldier. Although Brown got steady vitals, when the chief of surgery saw what he had done, he told Brown to remove the device and essentially, let the boy die. Colonel Brown refused and bullied his way to a spot on a C-17 aircraft headed to Landstuhl with other wounded soldiers. The boy survived, but Colonel Brown had to fight his way out of trouble.

Captain Davis, an Army chaplain at Walter Reed, followed Colonel Brown. Davis talked about death letters soldiers wrote to be opened only if they were killed in action. It was a good piece, as were his revelations about the life of a chaplain in Iraq. Last week, he wrote about how hard he tried to save a soldier from suicide but failed, a death that really bothered Davis because he thought he had talked the boy out of it. Davis also talked quite candidly during several of the sessions about how his wife was having an affair back in the states and had told him she wanted a divorce. Although Davis was a caregiver, he too needed help and the class provided him a safe place to vent, and in his case, a place to mourn.

Stories by other soldiers were equally powerful. Even so, one soldier's poem was so dark, I worried about the potential for suicide, looking to Stevens in shared concern. He silently acknowledged with his eyes that he would speak to the soldier after class.

Some soldiers just sat in silence, quietly nodding and leaving at the end of the class without saying a word. Others promised to bring something for the next class but rarely did. Walter Reed was a place you lived day to day.

Although I had taught writing at three North Carolina colleges, I focused this class more about getting feelings and emotions on paper than narrative arc, dangling participles, or even the thought of publication. Some of this stuff was just crazy, or sad, or, if it ever leaked, could be fodder for another Army scandal. It was probably too early, too close to the battlefield, and while satisfying for its participants, the group never got above six members at a time.

Starting the program was a challenge with little support and lots of rules and conditions. First, from my boss: It had to be after work, and it couldn't interfere with my job at the Pentagon. Second, from Walter Reed: Patients had to be cleared by their nurse case managers to participate. Many on the hospital staff were wary that soldiers writing and talking about their recent wounding might cause more pain than it would ease. I told the staffers that it was easier to write about the war than it was to talk about it, because talking sometimes brought on tears, and in the stoic culture of the military, you don't show your emotions. In writing, no one can see you cry. And if you do cry, you're among friends with similar experiences in a safe environment with a closed door.

After two months of meetings and emails with both medical and military leaders, Walter Reed decided to take a chance on me. In February 2011, they let me post fliers for the program on the campus. They also let me speak about the class to a group of about 200 wounded warriors at one of their weekly formations. Walter Reed leaders also allowed me to expand the program to include caregivers, several of whom had expressed interest.

I got the idea for the program at Walter Reed from my experiences in writing my 2004 book *Natural Born Heroes*, when I was surprised that many of the 55 World War II veterans I interviewed had never talked to anyone, family included, about the war. Collectively, their experiences were fascinating and touched every major event and personage of the war, from Roosevelt to Churchill, D-Day to Iwo Jima, movie stars to generals and even a future president. The common thread in *Heroes* was that they were all living in my 300-house neighborhood in North Carolina, and because I was both a neighbor and a veteran, they agreed to talk with me. From their stories I produced an oral history of World War II.

Yet until my individual meetings with these vets in their living rooms for several early evening hours, they were silent about their war. Once I got them talking, however, it was as if these events happened just yesterday, not 60 years earlier, with some of them crying about painful memories that remained with them in nightmares that were still all too vivid. At the end of the evening, they were relieved and thankful that, through my book, their families could finally understand what they did in the war and how it affected them before these stories were lost forever.

At the time of these interviews in 2002 and 2003, I didn't understand why so many of the World War II vets had never spoken about the events that shaped their lives at such a young age. That was until late 2008, when I also returned from war, in my case Afghanistan, and found what they found—no one was interested in hearing about the war and veterans needed to just get on with their lives.

Although my students at Walter Reed continued to write, a lot of the two-hour class was spent talking about the ongoing war. It struck me that during the day, in my job as a strategic planner at the Pentagon, I played a part in the planning of the war and on Tuesday nights, I saw the effects of that planning on these horribly wounded soldiers. Captain Stevens, who had been wounded in Iraq, told me that as the Army got better at saving lives on the battlefield, more soldiers, especially amputees, survived and populated the wards of Walter Reed. There they learned to use sophisticated prosthetics that almost, but not quite, made them whole.

All the wounded were treated as celebrities and people came up with other types of therapy, including fishing, art, music, and of course, VIP seats at ball games and NASCAR races. Some even came to the Pentagon once a month where the staffs lined the hallways three deep and applauded as the wounded, often with their families, began a tour of the building. Still, it was hard to watch and I found this "parade" of the wounded ironic because of the Pentagon's role in their injuries.

A highlight of my writing program was in May of 2011, when retired Army Lieutenant Colonel Ron Capps, who had visited my class at Walter Reed, organized an event for veterans to read from their works at Politics & Prose Bookstore in DC over Memorial Day weekend. This came as a result of Capps starting a similar but much more ambitious program that encouraged veterans of all wars to write about their experiences.

In September of 2011, the Army closed down the DC campus of Walter Reed and moved the service members and staff to Bethesda Naval Hospital in Maryland. During this shift, I stopped my program and let others, with Ron Capps' help, pick it back up once the transfer was complete later in the year. I had been reassigned from the Pentagon to the Arlington National Cemetery Gravesite Accountability Task Force in June 2011. In this new job, I led a team that corrected errors on records and headstones at the cemetery to make sure those interred there were properly commemorated. Sadly, we found thousands of errors, often misspellings and wrong dates, but also headstones that were misplaced or missing altogether. Compared with soldiers, however, headstones and records were easy to fix.

Captain Davis left active duty in late 2012, saying he was going camping and might be homeless for a while. I wasn't sure if he was kidding. Colonel Brown was medically retired in early 2013, but the Army never agreed that his illness was caused by the anthrax shots. Captain Stevens remains on active duty and continues to write. He also coordinated trips for Fatima to come to Boston for treatment of her burns and remains close to her and her family. Stevens' story about Fatima and Davis' story about death letters were published in *0-Dark-Thirty*, a military literary journal founded by Lieutenant Colonel Capps.

During a visit to North Carolina over Thanksgiving in 2012, I had coffee with Jeff Miller, a friend from my hometown, Hendersonville, North Carolina. In 2006, Miller founded HonorAir to honor his parents by sending all the veterans from Henderson County to see the newly completed World War II Memorial in Washington, DC. He then co-founded the Honor Flight network with Earl Morse, a physician assistant and retired Air Force Captain and pilot from Ohio, in 2007. By the end of 2014, the program had flown close to 150,000 veterans to DC from all over the country. The program has been featured on numerous national news programs, and Jeff and Earl received a Presidential Citizens Medal from President Bush in the White House in 2008.

During our coffee together, Jeff told me he was no longer doing HonorAir because he had taken all the Western North Carolina vets who were able to go to DC. He had found another passion, the Veteran's Restoration Quarters (VRQ), a homeless shelter in Asheville, North Carolina, that was exclusively for veterans. VRQ provided temporary and transitional housing as well as job training and counseling services. The parent organization, Asheville Buncombe Christian Community Mission, had purchased an old 240-bed motel complete with a full service restaurant to house this effort.

I found the idea interesting and Jeff's enthusiasm contagious, so I asked him to put together a meeting at VRQ. While there, I met the director and toured the facility, speaking to several of the formerly homeless veterans who lived, trained, and worked there. The place was electric with excitement that combined counseling and job training with a familiar military regimen that gave these fragile men structure and hope. After that visit, I got the idea to start another writing group there, similar to the one at Walter Reed.

With much less resistance than I found at Walter Reed, I was able to organize and support another group at VRQ. While all the participants were veterans, they typically were older, mostly Vietnam vets, although a few were recently discharged service members on hard times. Since I couldn't be there to run the program, I recruited two teacher volunteers and provided them with syllabuses, books, and advice. The class was launched in early 2013 to a group of regulars as well as drop-ins, who the teachers told me got into some pretty serious issues, much like those at Walter Reed.

I visited the group in September 2013 and watched and listened to the veterans' stories. They were heartbreaking and talked both of their war in the military and their war with homelessness. Still, I could see their enthusiasm for the class and felt that they, like the veterans in *Natural Born Heroes* and at Walter Reed, benefited from sharing their stories. For that I am glad. It helps me too.

TABLEAU
By Leni Berliner

One yellow lab
Two toddlers
Two café philosophers
Policemen in starched shirts
Patiently waiting for egg sandwiches
The light is still low
There is still a breeze
The Magnolias are still more powerful
Than the buses
July morning, Livingston & Connecticut, 7 a.m.

NONFICTION

GROW, CHANGE, THRIVE, BELIEVE

By Lisa Simm

It was the last thing I grabbed before leaving. Not much any-more, the plant was a few shoots with withering, dust-encrusted leaves. I removed it from the decaying woven basket that once was a vibrant, colorful housing for the pot. The pot, a durable green plastic, would last through the ages, way beyond the plant, me, or any of us.

As I stare at this potted plant that's by the kitchen window, on my Silestone countertop, I try to recall where it came from. Then I remember: My mother gave it to me 30 years ago.

It started as a plant clipping rooted in water. While growing up, I often witnessed roots springing forth and growing into floating webs of entangled strands. Sometimes the water got murky. Mom would gently rinse the roots, set them in fresh water; when the cut-tings were ready, she potted them. Now, in my kitchen, I imagine her filling the eternal green pot with soil, gingerly planting cuttings in the foreign land that would become home.

She gave me the plant when I moved from our home on Long Island to College Park, a huge university, a blue cinderblock room. She brought me there in a station wagon, to this brick place that was supposed to represent the beginning of the rest of my life. I spent most weekends visiting my high school sweetheart in Foggy Bot-tom, at GW, uninterested in finding a life of my own. I went home for the summer; the plant came, too. When I moved to an apart-ment in Greenbelt, the plant sat at my bedside. Next, my boyfriend and I rented a garden apartment in North Bethesda, within walking distance to the Grosvenor Metro where dwarf deer roamed unde-veloped land; the plant found a sunny spot on an old radiator in our bedroom. We lived there—the plant, my boyfriend-eventually-turned-husband, and I—for five or six years, attending GW's law school then working in DC as attorneys.

We had a daughter: A failed attempt at the Bethesda Mater-nity Center landed us at Shady Grove Adventist, a 27-hour labor.

The pregnancy deemed a pre-existing condition, my $7,000 hospital tab was then a hefty out-of-pocket expense. Instead of moving to Bethesda, we settled for Gaithersburg and a Muddy Branch townhouse that wasn't much. There was a kitchen bay window with hooks in the ceiling. This must have been when I bought the pink and green basket, its handle a rustic, curved branch. The plant hung in the kitchen, watched another daughter enter our family, the stress of being young parents, the choices made on purpose—or by default—about what this life would be.

I recall when we first bought this North Potomac five-bedroom "suburban-dream" colonial, the girls were five and three. We entered the vast, empty house to measure for curtains, furniture, the future. There was a bay window in the family room. The girls took turns sitting on the ledge that would become the plant's sun-dappled home. The plant stayed there, at the focal point of the family room, where I always noticed it, always remembered to provide the nourishment it needed: just water. One of the girls hid a plastic figurine of Cinderella's fairy godmother among the criss-crossing shoots and leaves. The plant thrived and grew, though the basket showed the first signs of fading.

Our second year in the house, the bay window became infested with carpenter ants, the wood rotted. Replacement was expensive, so we opted for a large picture window. Having lost its home, the plant re-settled on the fireplace hearth. It was chilly by the barren, twice-used fireplace. The plant did not grow or change, but it seemed content. I still remembered to water it.

I found it difficult being both a good mother and a good attorney. I knew I'd never regret staying home with my children. I was blessed with two precious daughters, connected to me by cords that were, by necessity, clipped. Over the years, keeping them safe, loving them, became a priority; protecting them as they journeyed toward becoming who they are was my primary focus. As their own roots grew, things sometimes got murky. I'd help them determine ways to change course, break from plans that weren't working, take chances, try something new. I helped them believe they could do that.

I took care of the girls and the home; he earned the money. He was the love of my life who cycled through being cold/distant and loving/attentive. Repeatedly, ridiculously, I was hopeful on the upswings. Year after year after year.

The home equity line was for emergencies, in case he became ill, if we couldn't save enough for the girls' educations. In case.

Somewhere along the way, his priorities shifted. With one daughter in college, the other a high school junior, he needed a kitchen remodel, wanted something sleek; thus, the maple cabinets, 52 square feet of Carrera Marble Silestone, hardwood floors, and stainless steel appliances.

We emptied the cabinets, the junk drawers, the pantry. I insisted on keeping the right side of the pantry door frame, adorned with pencil marks and dates: a reminder—maybe proof—of the many years' worth of growth I had cultivated here.

Due to construction debris, the plant took up temporary residence in a back room that once served as my part-time law office. The room was paper-cluttered, dusty, forgotten.

I supervised the tedious, painfully mismanaged kitchen remodel. What was supposed to take four weeks took four months—an ugly, unpleasant process with an inept, uncaring contractor. But the Silestone was beautiful, the maple cabinets impressive, the steel appliances gleaming. No more hand-drawn pictures or family photos affixed to the refrigerator with magnets; just sleek stainless steel unadorned by anything remotely familial.

The plant remained in the darkened office, forgotten. I forgot to water it, to lift the shades for sunshine. From time to time I'd see it while filing away papers. Nudged by mild guilt, I'd pinch off yellow and brown crumpled leaves, give it some water. It became smaller. Shrouded by thick dust, the surviving leaves were hardly green. By then the basket was straw-colored, the vibrant pink and green dyes gone. I left it there, turned off the light, closed the door.

No one is perfect. Married couples fight, bicker, go through changes, and I suppose the ones who get through it work quite hard to make that happen. But in my case, he would insult me. He would belittle me. He would make me feel small and crumpled, brittle and lifeless. No more "You're beautiful," no more hand-holding. No more. Now just a strange, silent marriage I didn't understand. I often wished to be dead.

But there were these lovely beings. Beings who were, themselves, growing and changing, but still needed me to guide them through murky waters, complications, overwhelming—sometimes devastating—situations. I had to be the stake that held them up. When they needed to hear, I love you, you're wonderful, you'll figure it out. You're strong, you can do it! Many mornings before they left for the (sometimes) cut-throat environs of Rockville's Wootton High School, their need for me was the main—really, only—reason I got out of bed. Now both off on their own, they need me still.

There was some home equity left. It was February when he proclaimed we must remodel the master bedroom and bathroom. His instructions were to make it "spa-like." We'd been through tough times: mental and physical health issues, disagreements, his jabs and insults dwelling in stagnant air (never softened or alleviated by "sorry"). The mounting emotional distance between us terrified me, so I gave him many passes. A lot of whatever you think, whatever you want. He wanted to remodel the master bedroom and bathroom. He wanted it spa-like.

I chose the materials, colors: Arizona Caliza porcelain tile, glossy stone accent tile, Caesarstone double vanity, chocolate espresso cabinets, oil-rubbed bronze fixtures, "butter pecan" paint. The hardwood oak I'd dreamed of for the master bedroom. It was a positive step for us, I thought, representing newness, a future where we could reaffirm our love and commitment to one another. It became an impressive space.

In April, I wrote the final check to the contractor. Within days, my husband informed me he thought of me as his child because I was pursuing a career as a professional writer and hadn't yet sold a piece. When he said it, I was on my computer at the kitchen table, fine-tuning my novel that I hoped would sell and help in providing for our family. "I'm your wife," I said, tears instantly streaming. More insults ensued. I shut down and—within days—became gravely depressed. Debilitatingly so.

More and more I sat on the couch, stared out the window, wished to be dead. For months. I was terrified to utter the word divorce.

Divorce happens to other people. We were special, different, had been together since high school. We were too codependent to get a divorce! But for years, he'd been going to functions without me, going on trips "alone" or "with the guys." Going, going, without me. It's true I got lost in cultivating the lives of my girls, in the characters who kept me company, in novels I was creating to share with others someday. I was at the kitchen table on my computer. I was staying; he, always, was going.

Throughout the summer he engaged in mind-warping games, leaving his wedding band on the Caesarstone double vanity, above the chocolate-espresso cabinetry, each day pushing the ring closer toward my sink, my side. He gave me the silent treatment. Everything I said was stupid. My requests for marriage counseling repeatedly were shot down, declined. I was the one with the problem.

My mind and body faltered more as depression festered. I wished I would die, already. Then, one afternoon in August, he returned from a trip and I looked him in the eyes: for a flicker of a second it was there, before he looked away. Guilt. Maybe pretend guilt. He wanted me to know what, perhaps, many already knew or had guessed. Something I never allowed my mind, at least consciously, to contemplate. I still don't know why that is.

I didn't want to die, really. I didn't want to take additional antidepressants, either. I needed to leave. In September, my 80-year-old mother flew up from Florida to help me load my station wagon. It was the last thing that I grabbed before leaving. While my mother waited in the car with my dog, I removed the plant from the old basket, blew off some dust, and looked around the foyer before closing then locking the front door. I stashed the plant in the back of the station wagon. It took 15 hours to drive from North Potomac to Lake Worth, Florida.

My parents helped me unload my belongings. My father hobbled, using a cane, and moved a vase so I had a place to set the plant: on an actual plant stand in the sun-filled loft outside the bedroom they'd lovingly readied for me. A safe, stable place to settle for a while. To untangle strangulating roots, to dust myself off and take a good look at what life had become.

I dusted each leaf, watered the plant daily. My parents showered me with love, made sure I was eating. They spoke to me! They ignited a small spark, made me believe I am still a worthwhile person. I have ideas to share, beauty within, and also—just maybe, still—on the outside, as well. They reminded me that three months after my husband said it was unlikely I'd ever be published, an agent fell in love with one of my novels and signed me on as her client. She's an industry professional—not my mother, sister, daughter or friend (but, perhaps, a fairy godmother)—who believes I can do this. I found a therapist in Florida, started weekly sessions. I passed the plant whenever I came to or left the bedroom; sometimes I'd talk to it, compliment it on its rapid, prolific growth. The open, airy loft, water, and a little conversation and encouragement were all it really needed. A safe place to settle for a while, where it sprouted new leaves, grew denser and richer in color, began to thrive.

In late October, my mother and I flew to DC for a writers' conference. Being plunked down amid the glorious amber, burnt-orange, and scarlet shades of a DC fall already in progress was disorienting, unsettling: For the first time in my life, I'd missed the prelude of chilling weather, the subtle day-to-day changes. It felt like loss.

With my mother, I returned to my home to retrieve a few items. The furniture was there, yet the house was ghost-like, vacant. After pondering a bit, she said, "This house is dead. You were its heart. It's an empty structure now."

He knew I'd be there and left clues. A half-empty bottle of rosé, two wine glasses in the dishwasher, her phone number repeatedly on the caller ID, condoms in his drawer.

I returned to Florida. He told my daughters of his plan to buy out my interest in the home. Ruminating thoughts of suicide became my constant companions, the image of holding a gun to my head, pulling the trigger, replayed on a loop. How did I get here? I wondered. I continued therapy; my parents somehow got me through the days. Then, all at once, the puzzling pieces came together: I had not chosen to leave my home. A choice between suffering a mental breakdown or leaving your home to survive, to escape years' worth of emotional abuse, is no choice at all.

I was forced out. There'd been a plan, maybe for quite some time. Maybe back to the time of the kitchen remodel, perhaps years earlier. He wanted leaving to be my idea.

I hired a lawyer, a private investigator. I told my husband I was returning to our home. He said it would be wrong for me to do so, it wasn't fair to him. The P.I. discovered not one but two women taking turns staying the night in my home, my bed.

My mother helped me pack the car on Thanksgiving Day. My father leaned heavily on his cane as he checked the air pressure of my tires. I'd reserved a spot behind the driver's seat for the verdant plant. It was the last thing I put in the car before waving goodbye to my father, staving off tears, driving back to reclaim my home, my dignity.

The signs reading "495 Washington" felt like "Welcome Home!" banners. When I pulled up to my house, I rediscovered strength I'd forgotten I ever had. A strength my mother saw when she left me in a lonely dorm room at UMD, where I was supposed to begin the rest of my life. I had plans, dreams and goals, and thought I had undying love. Plans and dreams change, paths veer in new directions, with unexpected detours. And love sometimes dies.

Upon entering the bedroom, I found the paramours' black and red hairs intertwined in the bed sheets. They were scattered on the Porcelanosa bathroom floor tile I'd liked so much for its subtle sparkles, in the extra-large shower accented with bronze. I went to the garage, got what I needed, and put up the Christmas lights.

It drives me insane thinking how I was "kept on" as an interior designer and project manager, then summarily dismissed, "let go," once the equity was drained, the projects completed. My husband had been preparing to share my home with a woman he'd been involved with for more than 15 years, beginning when she was a college intern at the law firm where he worked. "Red," the second woman, was for variety, nothing else.

I'm standing here, staring at the plant on the kitchen countertop—Carrera Marble Silestone. Ah . . . and there's another new leaf, in its early life, still curled in on itself, full of potential. The plant is reaching upward, standing tall. It's old for a plant, I suppose, but healthier, stronger, richer now than ever.

What I've done for my daughters, I'll now do for myself: make sure I figure out how to change course, break away from things that aren't working, not let history repeat itself, take a chance, try something new. Believe I can do it. Be a stake for myself when I feel like keeling over.

I've been through sheer hell battling this man. (That's a whole other essay—or novel.) But nothing about our relationship ever felt this right. By returning, standing up to him, I am triumphant. He'd carefully crafted a certain ending for our story: I rewrote it.

Goodbye dream colonial, images of daughters returning here for holidays with significant others, husbands, my grandchildren. The promise I made to myself? He would not remain here. He would not buy me out at fair market value and enjoy improvements from my equity. The house would be sold: Silestone, Caeserstone, hardwood floors, maple cabinets, stainless-steel appliances, bronze fixtures, porcelain tile, and all. We got an offer in two days.

Soon I'll transplant the plant. It's outgrowing the plastic pot, needs new space where it can grow, change and thrive. Me, too. For now, that's a rental in Gaithersburg.

The fairy godmother stays with us, wherever we go. That dollar-store figurine brings me joy, reminding me of two little girls, one of whom hid it there, and the fine women they've become: They've been there for me as I've been for them. It also reminds me of my parents, sisters, friends, agent, and therapist who believe I'll get through this even when I can't see how that's possibly true. They're all fairy godmothers, believing what I once thought impossible:

I'll be all right.

I almost believe it.

WISDOM

BROKEN CATHEDRAL

By P. E. Sloan

They say it's the coldest it's been
For at least twenty years
You look outside your frames
There's the National Cathedral
She's wearing a top hat
Scaffolding like wiry curls
Ringing the grand old dame
Propping her after the worst quake
Worst in a century they say

I was out taking a walk
When the plates shifted
Didn't feel a thing
Saw all my friends rushing out
Wondered if there was a new meth lab found
Something like that
Still though, really something
Cathedral and George Washington cracking
From the same fault

Time passes quickly now
We've been pondering Narcissus for centuries
The Cathedral cracked before selfie made it into Webster's
Yet was repaired before the selfie stick erupted
Before you could put your cloud-digit self
Right up against her injured façade.

IT'S COMPLICATED

By Korrin Bishop

I showed up late one night in August. I had driven all the way from California for this moment, and yet we just sat across from one another at the kitchen table, staring blankly.

Some places that I've traveled to I've fallen in love with immediately. Some cities have felt like best friends, while others have been passionate love affairs. When I arrived in DC, I wanted that type of feeling to overwhelm me. I wanted the city to sweep me off my feet. But it didn't happen that way. Instead, we sat across from each other at the kitchen table making small talk, asking the general questions you ask to learn the basics. Neither of us felt compelled to delve deeper.

Having studied public policy in school, I graduated wide-eyed, looking to effect positive social change. Doing time in DC seemed inevitable. I wondered whether this was why I felt shy upon our meeting. It felt too predetermined to be deemed an adventure. It was arranged, and we were going to coexist because we were living together now, but we didn't love each other. We would support each other as needed, and could only hope that over time we would learn to love each other, to gain love through a deep respect of sticking faithfully by one another's side through whatever came our way.

I grieved the loss of the West I had for so long called home. As a result, like too many millennials before me, I hunkered down and clung to the mindset that in a matter of one or two years, I'd be on my way. I held on tightly to this mantra even as other residents made comments that clenched my heart with fear.

"You blink," he told me, "and 30 years go by!"

It didn't take long before my shy beginnings turned into unadulterated loathing.

In an effort to grasp for all I'd known, I closed myself off to all that now was. Instead of opening my eyes to my present moment, I went along with society's preconceived paintings of what DC was. To support this defense mechanism, I wouldn't look for the city's beauties, but rather, I'd search for its ugly parts, for something to point a finger at and declare, "See! This is why it's ok for me to feel this way, to sneer, to disconnect."

In our nation's capital, I saw people experiencing homelessness on street corner after street corner. I saw a lack of affordable housing and living wages weigh heavily upon the quality of life of the city's residents. I read stories of extravagant parties held by lobbyists and an ongoing barrage of headlines on what Congress wasn't accomplishing.

Early one evening, I sat on the stoop of an office building, and watched a man's dog take a piss on the U.S. Government Accountability Office. I nodded in affirmation, and thought, "Touché, doggie, touché."

At happy hour, I overheard the judgmental conversations of young professionals—"I mean, she doesn't even have a five-year plan." I groaned in discontent over the rigidity of what seemed to be the region's socially accepted definition of success. It was a definition that left so many of us treading water just to keep up. I downed the last of my overpriced beer, and stumbled to the street.

"Go home, DC!" I yelled, "You're drunk!"

DC and I slept in separate beds that night—it, who knows where, and I curled up with my anger over my self-inflicted displacement.

It was a rocky start for DC and me, and a chilly winter, but scattered throughout, we did manage to make each other laugh from time to time.

Seven months into my DC residency, the weather started to warm up again, and life began to show that it still existed within the area's barren trees. I looked at DC, and DC at me, and we silently acknowledged that through the turmoil of the past months, we had each become different beings than those we were at the initiation of our relationship. We were spending more time looking into each other's eyes and actually seeing one another.

Although I noticed these changes, I was hesitant to get closer to DC, to commit to a place with no prescribed end date. But on a blue-sky day, it just happened.

I was minding my own business, exploring the area with two friends from out of town. The mid-70s weather relaxed my body and the light breeze playfully billowed out the bottom of my floral dress. We toured the Capitol building, visited where President Lincoln spent his last breaths, and squinted our eyes to try to make out words on the Declaration of Independence. When we stopped for brunch on Capitol Hill, it made me blush. In the spring light, DC's

115

eclectic row houses, park-like city roundabouts, and iconic monuments made something inside me giggle. I had to cover my mouth with my hand to hide my unexpected, secret smile.

It dawned on me—I had a crush on DC. As its delicate cherry blossoms began to bloom throughout the color pink's entire chromatic scale, so too slowly opened my own heart.

It didn't take long for my blue-sky crush to turn into unadulterated love.

I fell in love with DC because when I looked deeply into its eyes, I saw so much more than a city. I saw a dream in motion, an idea as a reality. Like all of us, it was riddled with imperfections, but it tried so hard to keep progressing. It was a place where anyone with a passion for an issue could come to give a voice to that cause. Through its very details, DC was teaching me what it meant to be a citizen of the United States and a citizen of the world.

DC seemed like a constant identity crisis, which bothered me at first. I couldn't pinpoint its style or attitude. But when I fell knee-deep in love, I saw that this was the point all along. I saw that DC was the actual identity of the United States. Its residents came from near and far. Some people had been in the city a long time, and others had just arrived. There was no particular color scheme. DC was always changing. Sometimes it let us down, and sometimes it led to revolutionary thinking. DC's identity crisis was a thin slice, a cross section of this big, wide world. It showed me how we were all lost and different, and yet united somehow in a drive to keep moving forward.

With its ever-abounding flocks of tourists, DC gave me endless opportunities to see it through its visitors' eyes—with that twinkle people have when they see something for the first time. I'd walk through the National Mall some days after work and see them, right arm stretched out as far as it could go, trying to capture a photo with the Capitol building in the background. It would make the ice heart they gave me during rush hour, as a result of their poor escalator etiquette, melt immediately. I recognized that the twinkle in their eyes was one we all need to bring into our work everyday—the twinkle that drove us here in the first place, back before we got too comfortable and too rundown to notice anymore. Unknowingly, these tourists gave me the gift of remembering how surreal it felt to become a part of something I had previously only read about in books.

However, unlike romantic comedies that roll the credits at this point, where everyone is happy and together in peace, my relationship with DC kept going. It couldn't always be this idyllic love, and although I ultimately knew that in my core, I began trying so hard to keep those moments of joy alive that it sometimes spoiled the whole.

Over the next three years, DC and I argued. We withheld affection. We needlessly tore each other down. Winters returned and froze our hearts.

The population of families experiencing homelessness skyrocketed at DC General Family Shelter. The government was shut down by the polarization and inefficiency of our elected leaders. Unreachable, high-end condo buildings continued to demolish preexisting, established senses of community.

Our relationship was tumultuous. After disagreements, we'd fall back into love with each other and try to pick up the pieces, but inevitably we'd miss a few. The cycle of love and loathe would begin again.

When I'd listen to the dialogue of others, to the news that tells us how to think, I'd swear off DC and resolve to move within the year. Later, I'd dig beyond the walls of transient millennial culture and I'd find perseverance, history, community, and love—the true pockets of what shaped the city. I'd see the real DC. It wasn't just corruption. It wasn't just a stopover on a path to something else. In these times, I'd cozy up in its arms and decide to stay a while. I'd rest there until I'd get restless, and then one of us would inevitably push away.

I stood on the National Mall one night, viewing glowing monuments blurred through teary eyes. Resigned, I whispered, "You're just a city of phallic symbols and the ghosts they leave behind."

Finally, DC and I decided to take a few weeks to think about us, to decide whether to part ways or to give it one last chance. We were both guilty of the same crime. During the hard times, we'd concentrate on each other's imperfections and try to lump one another into preconceived stereotypes of who we were. We should have been celebrating the depth and beauty of each of us as unique individuals.

Both bruised and scarred from each other's words, DC and I embraced. It wasn't over.

"Ok, let's just keep this rolling right along," announced the Metro driver over the scratchy train car intercom, and I smiled.

"It's all going to be ok," I thought. "Let's just keep this rolling right along."

I began to volunteer more hours in DC's eclectic neighborhoods with residents who had lived there for a long, long time. I started paddling the Potomac River, reading about its history as I sat

DISTRICT LINES

on its shores, and collecting trash as I went about, now feeling a duty to protect it. I learned about the places I saw and I tried to help out when I saw suffering. I felt privileged to know the side of DC that much of the country never gets to see.

Through this education and compassion, my love for DC has deepened tremendously, but it doesn't mean that our future is certain.

"Do you like DC?" they all ask when I tell them I live here now.

"It's complicated," I reply, "It has been turbulent. There has been love and there has been hate, but we've yet to reach a point of indifference."

DC and I are back to the kitchen table, re-exploring all of the things that evoked our passion for one another. We sit across from each other, now with years of shared feelings and stories, both well knowing that it might not work out. There may be a day I leave, and our conversations will cease. But perhaps, eventually, when it can forgive my late nights, my selfish asides, my lust for the other coast—and I its heartbreak, its broken promises of change, its obsessive silos—maybe then, just maybe, DC and I will learn to become just great friends.

For now, I hold on to my fervent love for a city that taught me how to grow.

THINK OF IT AS PAYBACK FOR YEARS OF RESTRICTIVE COVENANTS

By Debbie Levy

In the cemetery where my father lies,
Jews are toward the back, gentiles in front,
which puts the gentiles closer to the street,
which when Dad bought the plot
was a picturesque country road,
Georgia Avenue Extended,
which is now six lanes of traffic,
plain old Georgia Avenue,
which backs up during rush hour,
which never used to exist out here,
because this used to be farmland,
fields and churches and crossroads.

I'm not saying my father is crowing, but—
I imagine he is enjoying his peace and quiet.

NONFICTION

ESTATE SALE

By Jean Kim

I will never know this woman, but I am looking at her from the inside out.

The hallways have been stripped of their wallpaper, leaving behind wide abstract splotches of white paint upon pastel green. The floor is torn-up linoleum, laid bare from underneath vanished carpet. A sign points to the end of the hall, "Apartment 801, Estate Sale."

The door is barely open, and right away, inside the little foyer, I see piles forming.

In this cramped one-bedroom apartment in a Foggy Bottom, '60s-era elevator building, I've entered a manifestation of her brain, filled in every crevice and corner with collected memories. "Estate Sale" implies a placid mansion across serene manicured grounds. Here, it is a dusty, slipshod flea market, piles of knick-knacks, records and cassettes, remnant fabrics inside a heavy chest, stemware and glassware, souvenirs: an antique shop for one, or rather, a mini-metropolitan museum.

Her hunger for knowledge must have been voracious; volumes spill out of several shelves, mostly history books from many countries, a fair number in German or Spanish. Carved wooden facemasks hang across a window, paintings and posters range from Haitian art to silk Chinese zodiac animals. She documented milestones, with commemorative plates from the first Space Missions, or memorial coins from International Summits. And like me, she had a penchant for cutesy tchotchkes from her travels: Native American fetish animals carved from colored stone, painted Nativity scenes from Peru, Easter Bunny ceramics from Munich, refrigerator magnets galore, and a box of vintage postcards purchased and never mailed.

Everything is for sale; even her bedroom closet filled with silky robes and nightgowns, evocative of dated glamour, pink charmeuse to make a worldly old dame feel desirable. Her old hats, purses, snapshots of womanly pride. Her music is eclectic, everything from classical to jazz to world music, but decidedly not moving into rock and roll.

My friends pick some happy-looking Mexican ceramics, and I'm tempted by a small silver daguerreotype of a baby-faced World War I soldier, ghostly perfect in the reflected metallic surface. Being the child of immigrants who left everything behind in the 1970s, I have no claim to my own pre-war vintage collectibles, so such an old item fascinates me. I'm bewildered by this woman who bridged so many decades in history, so many travels, all inside her cozy capsule. I wonder what she did as a career: Was she a diplomat, traversing the world? Or a curator, a scholar, her curiosity being her most faithful spouse?

Ultimately, I feel uncomfortable taking anything out of this carefully compiled menagerie. It's a bit sad to see her history disassembled by legal necessity, cashiers at hand. She tried to carry her memories with her, in this madcap space, densely devoid of order but still loaded with life. There was something very modern, very DC of her, a woman ahead of her time, in the way she quested to explore yet possess the world from her American home base, using it as a point of international exchange and transience. The way she kept her inquisitiveness close to her heart; the way her rich mind hopefully kept loneliness at bay at the end.

I too hope to use my mind as fearlessly as she did, to collect the details of history, culture, art as a way to avoid isolation—to feel both deeply American and a citizen of the world, to still connect to people this way, even when you are sometimes left behind. Reminiscences reach out and travel into a stranger's soul—in my case, a woman from another era, another legacy—to breathe another day.

I walk back out of the apartment building into the busy city street, framed by monuments, into another rush hour.

CQMING QF AGE TWICE: AN ELEGY

By Richard Merelman

for Bob Porterfield,
Pitcher, Washington Senators,
1953: 22W-10L

Bob, in the dreams of my teens you're surpassingly handsome. You stand tall,
      Silence the Sox in the ninth, drag the impossible lugs—
Washington Senators—into the Series. You wave to the crowd, scrawl
      Autographs, pose with the bat boys. There are women who love
You for your sculptural torso, the flint in your grin, and your huge haul:
      Twenty-two victories. What's more, you are tough in the clutch,
Battle through injuries. Sluggers who thrill to the challenge of Fall ball
      Shudder when you're on the mound. Hollywood beckons; you shrug.

Finally, Bob, it's my day at the stadium. Only an off chance
      Places you close to my box seat near the end of the bench.
Breathless, I peer at you furtively, quiet as gravity. One glance
      Captures the river of snot shot from a nostril. I blench.
Later, you button your fly as you chomp on tobacco. A near-trance
      Follows. Or is it a catnap? You're immune to the stench
Strewn by the gas you expel. You distribute your spit as if priests chant
      Hymns to saliva; the dugout is perpetually drenched.

Now I am ancient; and Bob, you are dead as your time in the limelight.
      Here's what I've made of you: Trust facts, since the myths we forego
Never deserve to be honored. Your crudity? Honestly, just right;
      You disabused me of heroes. In their hubris, they sow
Sorrow: Achilles, Prometheus, Icarus, Hercules. Why fight
      Fate? When the '60's proclaimed *Change!* I responded *But no!*
Happiness lies in my Hyattsville bungalow. Recently, not quite
      Lively most evenings, I doze. Bob, you are back. And you glow.

TWO HILLOCKS AND A VALLEY

By Eleanor Heginbotham

O ne of my first books was inhabited by a family of four: the little girl had a pink bedroom; the dog had its own little house; the father smoked a pipe and said wise things; the mother was pretty; the baby, also pink, slept with a smile. The book became to me what blue eyes were to Morrison's Pecola: something lovely and unattainable. During World War II, my little family was missing the daddy. We lived in the California hotel my mother managed on behalf of the missing men in the family, and from that hotel, we wandered to some six or seven Army posts, where we lived in stuffy little houses that smelled of previous occupants until our father went away for the rest of the war and we returned to the three rooms plus bath in the family hotel. Thus, when the cheering stopped, the uncles and our father returned, and a Washington church called the Chaplain to be its pastor, we moved to what seemed heaven: Wesley Heights.

The Scottish wife of the assistant minister wrote my mother that our family might choose between a large house on Massachusetts Avenue (I wish I knew which embassy that house now is) or a house in the far suburbs in a new development. It was a shaded house, she said, on a nice lawn. In its front yard, she continued, the Scottish brogue coming through the letter, were "two hillocks with a valley in between." And so there were: little hills, but big enough for first adventures in sledding in the first snowfalls of our lives. On each hill were big trees that arched over the little valley between, just right for secret conversations between new friends. On the side yard, there was another little hill; the wall on that side had enough beige stucco to make a game of bouncing balls: bounce one, you turn around and catch the ball; bounce two, you throw the ball from under your leg; bounce three, you do something harder. The back-yard was too sloped for much play, but it merged into a wooded area that filled all the space between the houses all around the block. In addition to the big trees, roped with vines, one of which also had a

123

big rope swing that gave my friend a concussion, there was a little creek and a shallow pool. I offer these details because none of that exists now. This is the only way I can recover the faux tudor cross-timbered house that sat cater-cornered on 44th and Hawthorne, our home for 30 years. Now it does not exist.

That is not quite true. In the first place, while we lived there, it was not really our home; it belonged to the church. Elegant as it was, we were the poorer people on the block among neighbors who *owned* their faux southern plantation style homes and sweet Cape Cods. Second, although the house *does* exist some layers under the additions that have oozed out like grand goiters on all sides, the one with the 3001 44th Street address no longer exists. The church sold the property in the '70s, perhaps some owner thought 44th Street not a grand enough address. It is now a different number on Hawthorne Street. Why should that matter, especially now that other houses have taken their place in affection and memories? Somehow it does. When one has gone to school, having memorized the address of the first real home in childhood, when one has return-addressed hundreds of letters from that address, when that address has been almost sacred not only in the mind of the crotchety elderly woman writing this but in whoever is left who came to the parties in the manse, sat around the table, slept over on girlhood weekends, it matters that the address no longer exists. Imagine changing "1600 Pennsylvania Avenue" to some number on 16th Street: All of those families and their guests and tourists would be bereft too.

It was in or around 3001 44th Street, she says, making a mantra of the address while reliving memories: walking the seven blocks to Horace Mann School, kicking drying leaves or crunching on ice, knowing even then that some moments of those walks were epiphanies, moments of consciousness that were eight-year-old American versions of Proust's Madeleines, plotting or being surprised by birthday parties; shivering on the Cathedral Avenue corner where Santa Claus gave out gifts with individual names attached, then driving later that night around the neighborhood and nearby Spring Valley, awed at the all-blue or gold and green or spiffy white Christmas lights, and later, returning, sleepy, from the midnight service.

That 44th Street house she had run to when in trouble as a child, usually over small griefs but at least once in true terror. Laugh if you will, but she and her friends—school-children of the '50s who regularly saw the fierce face of Stalin on the front-pages of *Time* or *Life* or the *Post* or, in those days, *The Evening Star*—were convinced that we could be blown up. While continuing the war-time work of producing vegetable gardens during school recesses, they also took part in the duck and cover exercises and listened to their parents talk about what could happen if... One Saturday, early during the '50s in Battery Kemble Park, down the hill at the farthest reach of Wesley Heights, the siren blasted through the quiet woods. She was no athlete even then, but she had pumped those plump legs at sprint speed uphill for many blocks—to 3001 44th Street. No doubt, her mother had smothered a laugh or maybe she inwardly cried at the fear and the reason for fear, as she explained that the siren went off every day at noon as a test. There were other reasons to be embarrassed, some of them having to do with Miss Courtney's Dancing School above the grocery store next to Horace Mann, and some of them none of anybody's business.

The little girl matured and the house aged. Between her marriage in 1960, for which pictures show her leaving the arched front door of 3001 with sherbet pink-garbed bridesmaids and tuxedoed men, and perhaps a decade later she helped her mother clean out the house, beginning with its attic where she and friends had put on plays, and where, under its A-shaped bedroom—which was designed for maids but used by her—she had read more advanced books than the one with the little girl and her pink bedroom. In fact, that room had become alternately a place of prayer and religious thoughts at about twelve, and some four or five years later, a place of temptations with one male visitor (later husband).

She and her mother cleaned the dark reaches of the cedar-lined closets of the four bedrooms on the second floor, the unregenerated two bathrooms, where thousands of pages of magazines had been contemplated, and the broad room-sized linen closet, a dusty treasure trove. Together, they cleaned the dining room, which had hosted the entire congregation of a large church—split up by the alphabet or by the interest group (choir at Christmas, women in spring, and so on)—and the formal living room. Long gone, even then, were the two screened porches, one on the side closest to the street, site of late-night reads during the summer as the bugs batted around outside the screen, and one on the second floor, a tiny box furnished with Army-issue surplus bunk beds for sisters to share stories and questions and watch the fireflies light up the back woods. Something was lost when window air conditioners brought them all from the steamy summer to the artificial cold.

Below all of this was a house-sized basement, half of which held the washing machine that once came unhooked and danced

125

around. The basement also held a "mangle," which only a few will remember, and if they do, they will remember the sweet smell of wet sheets being ironed as one's mother put them through the treacherous, hot panels of this aptly named device. The other half of the basement is perhaps the most precious in memory. Paneled by the previous occupants (there had only been one other family there), in polished thick panels of oak (I think), it was lined with more of the Army surplus beds made into sofas and a few chairs all ranged around a plastic red and white, 12-inch TV box, at which, our father's protests notwithstanding, she screamed with the canned laughter at Uncle Miltie and Lucy and a talking horse. (I'm guessing that our parents had bought the set because they were embarrassed by our invasions—along with others in the neighborhood who did not have televisions—of those houses that could show "Howdy Doody" behind a big bubble that magnified the screen.) Years later, evacuated from Saigon with two babies and having returned to the safety of 3001 44th, this horrified then-young woman watched the war grow bloodier on a set only somewhat bigger—but big enough to invoke fear for her husband's safety as he had stayed behind.

Between those days and the cleaning out of the house and the inhabitation of 3001 44th by new people who took away its name and identity, my husband and I took advantage of a realtor's open house. We parked our grubby car several houses down on 44th and, dressed in church clothes, went through the house from top to bottom. Of course, to anyone else the changes would have been marvelous: On the ground floor, the dining room that had held so many guests had become a kind of entry hall to the new one, which was worthy of *Brideshead Revisited* if not "Downton Abbey." The kitchen, which was recognizable, led to a breakfast room that was not. Upstairs, an enormous master bedroom contained a small swimming pool for a swish bathtub and a walk-in closet; the old master bedroom had been cleverly re-fashioned, its ceiling removed to allow for a high stretch up into the eaves of what had been the storeroom next to the maid's room. Part of the storeroom floor had been retained as a loft over the old master bedroom, a little room big enough for a desk and chair and a terrific view up Hawthorne Street from the high window. The rest of the attic had also been refashioned wonderfully. As a girl, I had to stand on the bed to see from the window of the room designed for a maid. Now there was a huge window with another lovely view out over the trees of Wesley Heights. We learned that one of the owners had used the room for meditation.

Impressed, we descended to the basement, where all but one

thing had been "improved." My sister once had a boyfriend who fell in love not only with my pretty sister but also with Scotland, which he met through visits with us to Nova Scotia. He had painted up and down the open pipes of the basement thousands of tiny soldiers in varying tartan-patterned kilts, some with bagpipes, some with swords. There they were still in their original plaid colors, protected in the dark basement, product, thought the realtor, of a visiting artist. Well, yes, they were by a visiting artist, but we didn't volunteer our knowledge of his youthful, yearning self.

This older person is yearning herself—for the person who yearned for the pink room and the dog and the two parents. Along with those fancied figures of her first book, the actual parents have long since passed on: first to a spacious Westchester apartment; then to the assisted living rooms; then to the full care bed; then to the much smaller dwelling; and then—as her father would say—to "many mansions." The changed identity of the house is the smallest and maybe silliest of regrets in the necessary flux that changes the names of whole countries and whole cultures. Nevertheless, this outcast still savors the memories. Whether or not it is on her way to teaching gigs or board meetings or poetry readings, she still swings by what had been 3001 44th Street. The hillocks and the valley between them are long gone; in their place is a brick parking place rimmed with well-tended gardens. I hope that, buried as the old home is within that impressive new house, there might be a little girl in pink and a dog.

A BANQUET

By Michael H. Levin

(Finally, this wedding: Mayflower Hotel, July)

Each course a metaphor: Ripe
melons' curled prosciutto tongues.
Rare meats, sliced succulent with
hunter sauce. The sun-struck contours of
a lush gold peach. Dark melted chocolate,
suave as the woodwind section
of a summer orchestra.

Oaths may be good, but currents shift
while set meals have a place for
each—even absence, even sorrow.
So square the circle, beat the drum:
our bridegroom and dear bride, so
long delayed, have come
to sound a spell as old as flutes

in glades. Father Sky
and Mother Earth, bind them in the dance
of realignment and rebirth.
Like hawks and fishes, let them
find their lives in motion and in
holding still, and let them be
as wine in glass that glows translucently.

This table's our desire, our wish to them
for ease and wonder, joint surprise.
So as they tender love and launch
their craft, please grant us
grace, and pause yourselves:
alight; descend.
Partake.

NONFICTION

CUPCAKES AND CARDBOARD SIGNS

By Kate Reimann

W e burst into the ward apologizing for being late—"the traffic in Georgetown is terrible!"—but we have cupcakes and smiles and I suspect the nurses will be quick to forgive us—or rather, him. The nurses are always so fond of him. Probably because he always remembers their names.

"They're the ones who stick me with the needle—I don't need to piss anyone off before they do that," he explained with a smile and a shrug over a coffee at one of our other "treatment dates" while he reviewed their names from the Notes function on his iPhone in the Georgetown Hospital Starbucks.

His studies yield positive results—now the needle used to set up his infusions enters his pale skin as smoothly as it can into a bulging blue vein. He doesn't watch. Instead, he sits back in the overstuffed recliner, closes his eyes, flexes his forearm as the infusion starts, as if he can speed up the process of pushing drugs into the vein. But I understand this move as I sit on the edge of my chair, watching, vibrating with energy. Today is the last dose. He wants it done.

He opens his eyes and smiles at me, and we settle into our infusion-day habits of talking politics, talking about our kids, while the April breeze in DC fluffs the cherry blossoms beyond the window of the fifth floor, shaking snow-colored petals onto lush green-grass carpets below.

We still feel out of place here, the youngest patient and his younger wife on a floor full of tufted white hair and shuffling feet and snores. Old, wrinkled bodies whose insides betray them, curled up under warm blankets while the chemicals move through ports and into bloodstreams, killing in an effort to save.

Suddenly a familiar face peers around the curtain—my husband's first "cancer buddy" is in the next curtained room.

"I thought I recognized your voice," she smiles weakly at my husband but is ushered by the nurse back to her recliner to set up her infusion. She's receiving a big dose—though not her last. I sit with

130

her for a few minutes. She looks terrible, but I don't say it. There is no light in her eyes. I ask her about her kids. She tells me she's tired, she'd like to sleep.

She will die in six months. But we don't know this yet. I draw the curtain. I let her rest.

"She doesn't look so good," my husband whispers to me as he blows on his coffee. His worried face betrays his fear. I shrug, unwilling—or unable—to acknowledge the possibility of death that has mercifully evaded us so far. The sun so bright, the spring air full of promise. No, today death does not exist.

A friend from the oncology ward who runs the writing program stops by. She remembers today is his last day.

She throws her hands in the air in celebration and wishes him well. We chit chat—she will soon retire and delve into her novels and children's books—and I remember that we brought cupcakes.

"Take one!" I say as I force one on her, "We're celebrating!"

Soon all the nurses on the floor have a cupcake. They smile and lick frosting from their fingers and faces. There's laughter and commotion. I smile to myself as I observe the scene: a cancer party, with cancer friends and cancer nurses and cancer writing teachers. I used to push this life away, but now I embrace it. Now I give it cupcakes. But soon it becomes quiet again, our friend leaves, and my husband pulls out his laptop, and I pull out mine. The high of the cancer party has worn off, and now we just want it to be over.

Outside, lives move forward on busy streets beyond the hospital. Soon, I think, watching the cars drive by on Reservoir, soon it will be us.

Two hours later we are free—"We hope we never see you again!" the nurses say while shaking hands and doling out hugs—and we tumble into a beautiful April afternoon. We are giddy with happiness as we leave the hospital parking lot and turn onto Reservoir, lined with blooming tulip trees. My husband, rolling all the windows down, smiles, looks free. But we are immediately caught in Georgetown traffic, stopping in front of a perfect tulip tree only steps from the hospital. The sight takes me back to last year, to the infections, the smell of sickness, sterile hospital rooms. *I thought you were going to die.* I come crashing down from my high, the weight of it all—the cancer diagnosis, the fear, the exhaustion, the unknowns—settles on my chest. I can't breathe through the sobs.

He is belting out a song on the radio, waiting for me to join, when he notices me.

"What's wrong?" he asks. I can only stare at his left elbow, still wrapped from where they removed the needle.

The traffic begins to move again, but he doesn't notice, too busy wiping away my tears. The car behind us honks and we both jump. I begin to laugh.

"Nothing," I say as I dry my tears, blotting my cheeks. I pull down the mirror under the visor, rub away the mascara away from my eyes, pull the visor back up. I turn toward him, the tulip trees rolling by as we leave the hospital behind. "Absolutely nothing is wrong."

He holds my hand as he drives down Foxhall Road, dropping it gently to shift gears. We are at the height of rush hour, moving inches instead of miles. But he turns the radio up and sings along to an Imagine Dragons song as if he were alone on the road, as if he didn't have to shift gears every few seconds, as if he had never had cancer, as if he were free.

I'm on top of the world - hey!
I'm on top of the world - hey!

We creep down the incline where Foxhall meets Canal, and we see the man with a cardboard sign. The sign says he needs money, and he stands still when the light is green, approaches cars when the light is red. We brake. He starts walking the line of stopped cars.

My husband shifts his hips and reaches into his back pocket. He pulls out his wallet and grabs a wad of cash—I see tens and twenties in his hand. He folds his empty wallet, shoves it into his back pocket, settles back into his seat and waits.

The man stands at our car and reaches for the money my husband holds out to him. The light turns green as soon as the money is exchanged, and it's time to move. My husband looks forward, squinting into the sun, but I look back. I want to see the reaction.

The man with the cardboard sign looks into his hands. He drops the sign. "Oh, shit!" he shouts. "Oh, shit!" He's jumping up and down, then he stops. He throws his head back and shoots both fists straight up and screams "thank you!" to the sky. We laugh with delight as my husband drives us away. I see my husband glance into the rearview mirror one more time as the man with the cardboard sign starts jumping again on his small patch of grass between traffic.

"You gotta keep this good feeling going, you know? Gotta

spread that joy!" He bangs his hand on the steering wheel like a drummer with a beat and turns up the radio, and the wind and the sun and the song create a spring cocktail that goes right to my head. I'm dizzy with happiness, with life. I look at my husband: He is, too.

We drive faster now as the traffic scatters. I grab his hand. I sing with him:

And I know it's hard when you're falling down
and it's a long way up when you hit the ground
But get up now, get up, get up now

I'm crying again as we cruise over Key Bridge, the Potomac sparkling underneath us, the wind lifting the hair from my neck. But this time, it's with relief.

He's free.

And I know it's hard when you're falling down
And its a long way up when you hit the ground
But get up now, get up, get up now.

I'm on top of the world.

THERE, THEN HERE
By Rhonda Shary

for Lewis, Sylvie, and Tess

I.

Atlantic Ocean

    holder of souls

        before us crashing

        zipperlike along the line

            where the shore forms at this hour

            another place at other hours

            and drenched in silver moonshadow, rose-gold sunset light

A fine meal

    of gritty foil-wrapped packets

        chicken, yams, mushrooms, and sand

        yanked from the fire

            and they can't recall all the lyrics

            to all the songs they want to sing

        except for Graceland, still witty after all these years

Inhaling

    the rich pine smoke

        and wishing we still could see

        the seals who lolled out there only moments ago

            and watched us watching them, then dove

            and the blazing Summer Triangle

        obscured now by rolling ocean vapor and fire's smoke

Recalling

    that earlier hour

        of lavender sea now wine-dark and loud

        encroaching upon our small circle

            where our good dog, dozing, endures the smoke

            and the sand flies and the unpredictable waves

        for the sake of peacefully keeping her pack together

II.

When we first brought her here, she looked more confused than anything else, to tell the truth. This was a place never before been to but known in all its forms and shapes: rock, creek, forest. Here were a slew of new scents, and in wet mud, imprints of other paws and boots. Lifting her head, she surely heard, among the things we cannot ever hear, the steady thrum of rubber on roads too near this oak aspen maple and beech, all grown fragile from the strain of withstanding this onslaught, this forced change from without, this strange exhaust, tenuous roots, against centuries of event not ours—taxing an old dog to learn new tricks.

III.

She had come with us at her last,

    when we, displaced by others' decisions,

    landed in the place most densely-

    populated-by-NYkers outside of NY

    and only when the routine

    of work and walks took root

    did home begin to happen again

    then, on those snowy late night circuits

    amid the muffled quiet of the powdered courtyard

    and the paw prints and boot marks of others

    would her age fall away, and unburdened animal joy rising

    in a spiraling four-point take-off,

    leapin and a-hoppin like a well fleet pup

        —in that moment perfectly alive,

    a perfect arc against the raw tides

CONTRIBUTOR BIOS

Leni Berliner — *Tableau*

Leni moved to DC for a job in 1980 and didn't leave after five years as planned. Leni has had two careers and is now a painter. Anything (in the way of paid employment) considered.

Korrin Bishop — *It's Complicated*

Korrin L. Bishop is a California native, Oregon Duck, and current resident of Washington, DC, where she works on local and federal initiatives to end homelessness. In addition, she is an essayist with publications in *Shelterforce Magazine* and *Misadventures Magazine*. You can find more of her writing on her blog, Rough Outlines, at *www.roughoutlines.com*. Her writing generally focuses on the intersections of people, place, and community.

Gabriella Brand — *Flight Pattern: Zackary*

Gabriella Brand's short stories, poetry, and essays have appeared in a variety of publications including *Room Magazine*, *The Christian Science Monitor*, *The Binnacle*, *StepAway*, and *Perigee* as well as several anthologies. She is a Pushcart Prize nominee and a SpiritFirst Editor's Choice winner. She lives in New England, but her family lives in DelRay, Alexandria, Virginia so she knows the District well. You can find her work at *Gabriellabrand.net*.

Gina Brown — *Rush Hour*

Gina Brown is a writer who questions the questions and elicits even more questions through her writing.

Sally Canzoneri — Photographer

Sally's photo appears on page 9

Sally Canzoneri is a photographer, book artist, and writer. Her artist's books and photographs have been in numerous juried group exhibitions, and her articles for adults and children have been published in a variety of magazines. Recently, she has had solo shows of her photography at ArtSpace DC and at The Hill Center at the Old Naval Hospital. Sally lives in DC with her husband, daughter, and "the cutest three-legged dog in the Western Hemisphere."

Matt Finkelstein — *Farewell to the Fight*

Matt Finkelstein is a speechwriter by day and is pursuing his MA in nonfiction writing at Johns Hopkins University. His work has appeared in the *Washington Post*, *The Daily Beast*, and *Esquire*, among other outlets. He lives in Washington, DC with his wife and son.

Susan Mann Flanders — *The Dog Park*

Susan Mann Flanders is a retired Episcopal priest living with her husband, Bill, in Northwest Washington, where they structure their lives around morning and afternoon dog park excursions. Susan's recently published book, *Going to Church: It's Not What You Think!*, weaves together her life as a priest, wife, and mother as she addresses questions about faith and the future of church and why they matter.

Willa Friedman — Photographer

Willa's photos appear on pages 25, 43, 75

Willa Friedman has had solo shows of her photography at 1st Stage Theater near Tysons Corner and Waverly Gallery in Bethesda. Her work has also been shown recently at the Art League in Alexandria, Photoworks Gallery in Glen Echo, and Art at City Hall in Alexandria. She also has work in the permanent collection of the Center for the Photographic Arts in Gainesville, Virginia and various private collections.

DISTRICT LINES

Renee Gherity — *Under the 14th Street Bridge*

Renee Gherity has lived in the DC metro area for the last 23 years. Her work has been published or is forthcoming in *Poet Lore*, *Innisfree Poetry Journal*, and *0-Dark-Thirty*. She is a participant in the Writer's Center's Ekphrasis Project, opening winter 2016, which pairs the work of painters and poets. Renee has given readings in Minnesota, DC, and Maryland.

Tara Hamilton — *How the Nation's Airport Came to be Closed for 23 Days*

Tara Hamilton is a native Washingtonian who attended schools in the District of Columbia and taught at Ballou Senior High. Her career path led her to public service with the District government and then with the Metropolitan Washington Airports Authority, where she served as the public affairs manager for 21 years.

Deborah Hefferon — *Wildflower Walk*

Deborah Hefferon is an independent consultant working in the fields of international education and cross-cultural training. Her personal essays have appeared in such publications as *The Pen is Mightier than the Broom*, *The Christian Science Monitor*, and *Potomac Review*. Her poems have found homes in local publications, including *District Lines, Vol. I* and *Prospectus*.

Eleanor Heginbotham — *Two Hillocks and a Valley*

Eleanor Heginbotham raised a family as a Foreign Service wife in Liberia, Vietnam, and Indonesia, where she also taught. She has been a lifelong learner, earning her "terminal degree" after age 50, doing so as she taught full-time at Stone Ridge in Bethesda. In retirement from a tenured position as a professor at Concordia University-Saint Paul, she continues to publish on Emily Dickinson (two books and dozens of articles), to lecture, and to teach at OLLI. Some of the rest of the story is implied in her little memoir of a home, included in these pages.

Kelly Ann Jacobson — *Snow Day in Washington*

Kelly Ann Jacobson is a fiction writer, poet, and editor who lives in Falls Church, Virginia. She received her MA in Fiction at Johns Hopkins University, and she now teaches as a professor of English. Kelly is the author of several published books, including the novel *Cairo in White*. Her first book of poetry, *I Have Conversations with You in My Dreams*, will be published by Alabaster Leaves Publishing in February of 2016.

Sally Murray James — *Fireboat on the Anacostia*

Sally Murray James is an Eastern Shore native who moved to the District for the weather, after the meteorological shock of a New England education. Her poems have appeared in *Washingtonian* and *The Hill Rag*, and an essay she cowrote with her sisters appears on the Yale AIDS Memorial Project website. She works as a graphic designer at Dupont Circle and lives in Southeast with her partner, their daughter, and a pet snake.

Bob Johnson — *Tuesdays at Walter Reed*

Bob Johnson is a retired Army Reserve officer and veteran of Afghanistan. Author of two books, he recently received an MA in Writing from Johns Hopkins University. Bob lives in Washington, DC and is a writer at the Office of Inspector General of the U.S. Department of Housing and Urban Development.

Zoe Johnson — *"When Sorrows Come"*

Zoe Johnson is a young writer from Silver Spring, Maryland. In addition to all things Shakespeare, she enjoys learning languages, biking, and going on adventures.

Cary Kamarat — *Miss Kitten at Alley Blues*/Photographer
Photograph appears on page 69
Cary Kamarat's poetry has been published in *District Lines, Vol. I*, *The Federal Poet*, *Poets on the Fringe*, *Prospectus: A Literary Offering*, Israel National Radio, and *First People: Native American Poems and Prayers*. His photography has appeared in *District Lines, Vol. II* and *The Tulane Review*. A debut collection of his poems and photographs, *Travelwalk*, was published last year.

Leah Kenyon — *Please Come Back*
Leah Kenyon was born and raised, by wolves, in Washington, DC. She has her pack's blessing for this, her second essay in *District Lines*.

Jean Kim — *Estate Sale*
Jean Kim is a physician and writer currently working and living in the DC Metro area. She received her MA in Nonfiction Writing at Johns Hopkins University, and has also been a nonfiction fellow for the Writers' Institute at the Graduate Center of CUNY. She has been published or is forthcoming in the *Washington Post*, *The Rumpus*, *The Manifest-Station*, *The Daily Beast*, *Bethesda Magazine*, *Storyscape Journal*, *Star 82 Review*, *Little Patuxent Review*, *Gargoyle Magazine*, *Niche Literary Magazine*, and more.

Debbie Levy — *Think of It as Payback for Years of Restrictive Covenants*
Debbie Levy is the author of more than 20 books for young people, including *The Year of Goodbyes* (Disney-Hyperion); *We Shall Overcome: The Story of a Song* (Disney-Jump At The Sun); *Imperfect Spiral* (Bloomsbury); and the forthcoming picture books *I Dissent: Ruth Bader Ginsburg Makes Her Mark* (Simon & Schuster) and *Soldier Song* (Disney-Hyperion). Debbie has lived in the DC area her whole life.

Courtney LeBlanc — *Follow the White Rabbit*

Courtney LeBlanc believes wine, coffee, and poetry are key ingredients in life, though she's always tinkering with the recipe. Her poetry is published or forthcoming in *Connections, Welter, Plum Biscuit, Pudding Magazine, NoVa Bards Anthology, The Legendary, Germ Magazine,* and *District Lines*. Read her blog at *www.wordperv.com*, follow her on Twitter: *www.twitter.com/wordperv*, or find her on Facebook: *www.facebook.com/poetry.CourtneyLeBlanc*.

Michael Levin — *A Banquet*

Michael H. Levin is a lawyer, solar-energy developer, and writer based in Washington, DC. He has published poems in *Adirondack Review, Midstream, Poetica, The Federal Poet,* and *District Lines,* among others, and has received numerous poetry and feature journalism awards. His collection, *Watered Colors* (2014), was named a "Best Book" of May 2014 by the *Washington Independent Review of Books*.

Fiona J. Mackintosh — *Jericho Road*

Fiona J. Mackintosh is a British-American writer based in the DC area. Her essays and features have appeared in the *Washington Post, American Heritage Magazine,* and *Bethesda Magazine*. Her short stories have been published on both sides of the Atlantic and have been longlisted for Plymouth University's 2015 Short Fiction Prize and the Heekin Group Foundation's Tara Fellowship in Short Fiction. Her story "On Warren Ward" won the TSS Flash Fiction Competition in November 2015. You can follow her on Twitter @Fionajanemack or on her blog, called Midatlantic: *http://fiona-midatlantic.blogspot.co.uk/*.

Richard Merelman — *Coming of Age Twice: An Elegy*

Richard Merelman, a native Washingtonian, grew up in the Mount Pleasant neighborhood. He taught political science at the University of Wisconsin-Madison (with brief periods away) for 30 years. His poetry has appeared in journals and in his first book, *The Imaginary Baritone* (Fireweed Press, 2012). *The Unnamed Continent*, a new poetry chapbook, will be published by Finishing Line Press in 2016. He and his wife live in Madison, Wisconsin.

Alexa Mergen — *The Reflecting Pool*

Alexa Mergen's poems appeared most recently in *Axe Factory* and *Virginia Quarterly Review*; her latest chapbook is *Winter Garden* (Meridian, 2015). She's a private yoga teacher specializing in home practice for increased clarity, strength, and harmony. Alexa also offers small-group instruction in meditation and poetry to people of all ages and experience.

Natalie Murchison — *Sunset Liquor*

A sixth-generation Texan, Natalie moved to DC when she was 18. From Georgetown to Columbia Heights to Bloomingdale, Natalie has spent the past 10 years navigating adulthood in Washington. When she's not writing—third-person bios or otherwise—Natalie works for a software development firm, managing open source projects for nonprofits, and volunteers for a female empowerment organization, femex.

Patricia Aiken O'Neill — *Genetic Imprints: The Color of my DNA*

Patricia Aiken O'Neill moved to Washington, DC as a young child, graduated from local schools, worked in Washington as an attorney and association executive, and retired in Chevy Chase, in 2012. She has written professional and personal essays and poetry for publications including the *Washington Post*, and most recently, "A Little Rock and Roll and A Good Cigar" appeared in the first volume of *District Lines*.

Erin Page — *To-Do List*

Erin Page is a writer living and working in the Washington, DC area. Her first publication was a folk-fairy tale adaptation in *Mytholog*. She blogs at *ErinPageWrites.Tumblr.com*.

Kate Reimann — *Cupcakes and Cardboard Signs*

Kate writes personal essays, op-eds, and speeches. Her work, "Masking Tape," was chosen for last year's volume of *District Lines*. She lives in Alexandria, Virginia with her two boys and her happy husband.

Lena Rothfarb — Photographer

Lena's photos appear on pages 84, 111, 113
Lena Rothfarb is a senior studying linguistics and Spanish at Georgetown University. Originally from Bethesda, Maryland, she is a long-time lover of Politics & Prose, but is still confused about when exactly she outgrew the kids' section.

Melody Rowell — *Saturday Night: Jumbo Slice*

Melody Rowell lives in Washington, DC, where she works as a photo coordinator at *National Geographic* magazine.

Karen Sagstetter — *Afternoon in Arlington Cemetery*

Karen Sagstetter has been published in more than 40 literary journals, two chapbooks of poetry, two nonfiction books, and *The Thing with Willie*, a collection of linked stories. She studied in Japan as a Fulbright journalist, was head of publications at the Smithsonian's Freer and Sackler Galleries, and senior editor at the National Gallery of Art.

Emily Sernaker — *After the March*

Emily Sernaker is a writer and activist living in Washington, DC.

Rhonda Shary — *There, Then Here*

Rhonda Shary's poetry has been published in *The Shawangunk Review*, *WaterWrites: A Hudson River Anthology*, and *A Slant of Light: Contemporary Women Writers of the Hudson Valley*, among other journals. A former adjunct professor of literature and writing, and long-time resident of New York City and the Hudson River Valley, she is now in DC working at Politics & Prose, where she is coordinator of the Book A Month program.

Lisa Simm — *Grow, Change, Thrive, Believe*

Lisa Simm has made the DC metro area her home for more than 30 years. She writes novels for the adult and young adult markets, and is working on an early chapter book series.

P. E. Sloan — *Broken Cathedral*

P. E. Sloan is a writer and civil servant living in Northern Virginia. He has worked as a journalist in Connecticut and Florida, and along the way, he has lived in Chicago, Brooklyn, and Paris.

Harold Stallworth — *64 Squares*

Harold Stallworth is a structural engineer living in the Del Ray neighborhood of Alexandria, Virginia. His writing has appeared in *Washington City Paper*, WAMU 88.5's "Bandwidth," *The Bookends Review*, and *Passion of the Weiss*, among other places.

Vanessa Steck — *My Manic Pixie Dream Girl*

Vanessa grew up in DC and as a child had access to a charge account at P&P, which nearly bankrupted her parents. This piece is dedicated to her father, Robert Neille Steck, whose service in Vietnam ultimately led to his death; before that, he bought a great number of books about the subject at Politics & Prose, including once when he was on his way to the ER. She is currently at work on her second novel. Find her at *vanessasteck.com*.

Lee Sturtevant — *Go Fish*

Lee Sturtevant lives in Cleveland Park and writes about local history and landmarks. Her biography of turn-of-the-century banker, philanthropist, and park-promoter Charles Glover will be published soon.

Jennifer Kline Vallina — Photographer

Jennifer's photos appear on the cover, the back cover, and page 21
Jennifer Kline Vallina has been taking photos since she was 10 years old and has spent more than 30 years capturing the beauty of the world overlooked. She finds intricate patterns and mesmerizing detail in objects that we walk by every day without a second glance; her work attempts to bring a consciousness to the invisible, yet amazing landscape that surrounds us.

Kris Weldon — *In My Pocket to Keep*

Kris Weldon has lived in Tokyo, Nanjing, Seoul, and a very small town of little consequence in New Zealand. She is a graduate of Temple University, where she studied Japanese and spent entirely too much time in the library writing fiction instead of studying math. Her works have appeared online at *Imminent Quarterly* and *1000 Words*.

Pamela Murray Winters — *Shy Supplicant*

Pamela Murray Winters, a lifelong resident of the DC area, has had poems published in the *Gettysburg Review*, *Gargoyle*, *Beltway Poetry*, *Fledgling Rag*, and the anthology *Takoma Park Poets 1981*, among other publications. She lives on the western shore of the Chesapeake.

Rob Winters — *Motorcade*

Rob Winters is a DC-area native and a computer engineer at NASA Headquarters. He is married to a poet and participates in poetry events in the DC area and Annapolis. He lives on the western shore of the Chesapeake Bay in Churchton, Maryland.

Anne Harding Woodworth — *In the Bishop's Garden*

Anne Harding Woodworth is the author of five books of poetry and three chapbooks, with a fourth, *The Last Gun*, appearing in early 2016. Her work is widely published in literary journals in print and online in the U.S. and abroad. She lives in Washington, DC, where she is a member of the Poetry Board at the Folger Shakespeare Library.